In praise of *The slant hug o' time*...

"Playfully earnest and pleasantly baffling, *The slant hug o' time* is a work like no other. Enabled by rhymes, puns, anagrams, science, pseudo-science, reason and unreason, it joyfully elides the past, present, and future, along with (I believe) new time zones yet to be discovered. In other words: it's a slippery world out there, and welcome to it."

—Jim Krusoe, author of *Toward You*, Tin House Books

"In its manner of telling, *The slant hug o' time* mimes ENTROPY. Time 'just spirals back on itself, like a rhyme.' Smith plays with time (as he plays with language) and time plays with his characters. Everything goes to pieces before the Gates of Pearl or Peril... Nabokov's Ada meets V[onnegut]'s Billy Pilgrim, swinging about in maybe parallel worlds and jigaboo time."

—Tom Smith, author of *Jack's Beans: A Five-Year Diary*, Birch Brook Press

"...the shadow of Gertrude Stein here, but without the 'look how original I am' posture."

—Lee Byron Jennings, artist, author of *The ludicrous demon: aspects of the grotesque in German post-Romantic prose*, University of California Press

For Kathryn Jacobs – one of our all-time favorite artists. May your life be filled with hugs!

love Don Smith
26. vii. 2012

The slant hug o' time

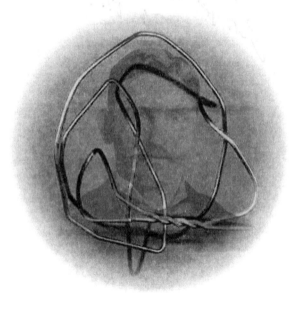

The slant hug o' time

George Drury Smith

Kitsune Books

Quality books for eclectic readers

The slant hug o' time

Kitsune Books
P.O. Box 1154
Crawfordville, FL 32326-1154

www.kitsunebooks.com
contact@kitsunebooks.com

Printed in USA
First printing in 2012

ISBN-13: 978-0-9840058-1-9
Library of Congress Control Number: 2011944956

Front and back cover design: William K. Morosi
Author photo portrait: Kathryn Jacobi
Inside graphics: George Drury Smith and William K. Morosi

First edition

Acknowledgments

I would like to thank James Krusoe and Fred Dewey for priceless help and suggestions which led to the current version of this novel, as well as my partner Leston Chandler Buell and my friend William Keith Morosi, among others, for their support and encouragement.

In memory
of
my dear friend and colleague
Alexandra Garrett (1926-1991),
who encouraged and supported so many writers;
and
my high school teachers
Sarah Zimmerman and Mary Crawford,
who fostered my bizarre creativity
and allowed me to go in strange new directions
those many years ago.

Dedicated to
English teachers everywhere.

Table of Contents

Editor's Note

What follows is excerpted from a curious and possibly unfinished or fragmentary document entrusted to me to abridge and prepare for publication, perhaps because the publisher views me as just as pedantic and cantankerous as the author, whom I know only as "D."

This thankless editorial task is complicated by my having also been furnished with a version of D's unpublished so-called "Mémoires," which parallel but differ substantially from the poetic and perhaps more factual work at hand. The best outcome might have been to publish the two works together and unabridged, perhaps on facing pages of the same volume, but I have hesitated to suggest this, as it would have required a monumental, if not impossible, effort of correlation and concordance, and would as well probably have detracted from the otherwise general appeal of the present work, especially in view of the fact that it was meant to be read aloud.

The material varies widely, and indeed wildly, in style, point of view, provenance and genre, including sections of personal correspondence and other documents, reminiscences and lyrical —sometimes prurient—reveries.

I have attempted to arrange this sometimes disconnected material in a somewhat logical if not totally linear order, but have made few alterations to the text selected, and suppressed no material essential to the story, except a few passages in the interest of protecting the living and the memory of the identifiable dead. Such omissions are indicated by: [...xXx....].

Attempts to clarify obscure passages or words are rare. Also, most of the sometimes absurd and sometimes prescient scientific and metaphysical observations have been retained without comment.

In the early part of this manuscript, D seems intermittently to be drawing from correspondence (which he never dates) that he claims to have had with Sarah Spiderman Siegfried (also referred to as Sarah, Sarah Spiderman, Sarah Siegfried, S, SS, Sar or Cookie), one of his high school English teachers. Due to similarities between the style of Sarah's letters and D's own, we are led to believe that the former have been heavily edited by D.

Though Sarah had been D's mentor and even confidante through his apparently troubled adolescence and early manhood, he lost touch with her when he was in his even more-troubled mid-20s, only to reconnect with her quite accidentally (perhaps in the 1960s or later) when he was starting research for a biography of his grandfather, George Ludwig Haasen, which inspired this memoir. The correspondence apparently lapses, or perhaps is simply no longer referenced, as D grows more familiar with the events here treated concerning the first half of the 20th century and starts to be aware of the immense power that Sarah eventually wielded in the second half and well into the New Era.

—*Gregory Hirsute, MD*
at Holywood, Suda Kornukopio
Aztlanafedo 34.08WNH 118.37
27th Fluember, New Era Year N-9

PART I

Chapter 0

Introduction

On those barren New York landscapes,
back then on the eve of the Year Delta of the so-called
Interstice or Interspell,
that interstitial period between the Old and New Eras,
after that sliver there between Central Park and the East
River had been razed, replaced and rephased;
and when abandonment was imminent of what had been
plotted out as the New Mews-Manhattan Emerald Gardens
Project for dazed and crazed night-rap red-mare dreamers and
unfazed reed rammers; and
after queer fear had, again, disappeared
even beyond the cheerless, charred frontier and
the banks and strands of what we called "North,"
and the wires and cables were cut thenceforth
even to Fire Island not-far-afield
(where they'd once planned to ban
the oddest of the immodest sodomite idols
who'd been grabbed and nabbed for Bridal Sin)...
on one of those strange, lonely promenades we dared,
in the fantasy-fields we shared,
shielded among phantasmal Hades-head shards,
shaded among the sheared
blood-red towers and
cadmium-yellow steel and concrete monsters

still slyly stretching
to a sky of bland white background
and purple-blue teardrop clouds,
after sunrises of slate-blue peach...
in the blazing rays of those dawning days,
which are so real and clear
in this finale-fling of my racing, reeling memory,
when along breezeless risen seas,
among ruined leafless summery trees,
Sarah Spiderman Siegfried would take me and C
in her horse-drawn pseudo-trolley galloping east
over towards that purported North Pivot,
before the predicted rip and breach of the dikes and
final attempts to avert the
long-feared imminent submersion that led to the
the Second Great Tramontane Dispersion to the West...
yes, then, I came to know we were
Part of It All.

Ha! The shifty new-hewn "North," fingered and marked by that once anointed and precise old magnetic pointer device, is now a thorny folly, indeed.

"The compass still works," Sarah would say in pathetic rejoinder, but we—and she—knew it could not, for not only had she unapologetically skewed the deviation tables of the already peripatetic magnetic North Pole before West seemed to go to the Lodestar, and twained trails met, she was also able to contrive a rift, to shift the global pole itself so that her own Alteranet and other secret systems could be centered someplace near the Big Apple fret.

But now, as earth's bipolar leitmotif groaned under pathetically and died out, blown asunder, in what zone had Sarah newly re-sown the seed of the leading lodestone?

So, in response to the recent insidious destruction, pervasive and orgiastic alteration, distortion and drastic reduction of

historical source materials relating to our place and age and indeed to all other times and climes,
    I've been asked—and accepted
    with no little reluctance and humility—
    to undertake this task and unmask and disclose
    in this Year N-7 of the New Era
    some fascinating partly third- and fourth-hand reports
    of events that led straight
    to this latest state of affairs.

And in this, my perhaps last gasp, I will no longer masterfully conceal some of my own thought-lost past, opting instead to shed it here, and retell and reveal every shred of it clearly,
    (nearly)
    spread it all out on these unstable pages—Still paper, you say?—far beyond the pale of all the flawed and ailing awful old Internet babble and the baleful tangle, ebbing and failure, and long after the at last unstable wobble of that fabled World Wide Web and cable.

So I'll attempt to preserve and bequeath to you readers in the home reserve some of the history that was hidden beneath and behind the unnerving, fallacious, specious and self-serving "controlled data" that permeated the contrived and hated so-called "cyber-force" beta sources that now disgracefully replace, efface and erase beyond all grasp the wise old surreal-jive literature blur that once so thrived before those rickety hard-disk-drives and later electromedia and optico-molecular bioblips and nanochips arrived inside the high-arched hives and sacred arks of our great old libraries and archives.

Thus, in my own baroque,
    mock theta-wave-stoked,
    smoke-and-rave,
    hot-and-cold,
    in-and-out bold auntie dance
    and pre-plotted anti-pedantic
    alto-chant edict-style stance,

I yearn to discourse on what I've learned about the
primeval moving forces and evils in some of the recent
world political and even geophysical upheavals
when those nasty plush-phase
lackeys of the old Presidential Dynasties raged,
—unleashed and quick to shoot—
lashed out, and crushed and shattered
for many of the masses
that vast and unsurpassed old pattern
of Alpha to Omega
and writin' and readin',
and later reduced Knowledge and Learning
to now-Net-infected drivel.
So, I would denounce the war nuts down to their roots,
renounce and rout out the untrue eco-con duds,
sift and sieve through that sick-Net stuff,
thrash the fluff and trounce the chaff
down to the kernel,
cull out and collect the Truth,
and write down and recount it all here in this journal.

Ohio is where I come from, so this tale starts in the Eastern
Midwest, with some original, earthy and outwardly mundane
iconoclasts who each, under the mantle of innate and humble
simplicity, quietly wielded the awesome powers that led to the
short-lived New Mews-Manhattan and its ultimate fate. And
they incited the demise of our USofA, indirectly inspired the Rise
and Dominance of the Old West after the Second Tramontane
Dispersion, stirred and spurred the rest of world as well to rebirth
and perhaps even helped save the earth.

Oh, my, O-hi-O, then bounded (in undistilled child-
thought) in the Maumee headwaters by Aunt Till, who lived east
of West Cairo (rhymes with Pharaoh);

on the South by the Ohio River;

on the east by the west Allegheny brim, Blennerhassett and

Marietta;

then on the North rim by that Giant Rubber Tire that sticks in my mind, the Blue Hole and what is now the Erie *Subkonfedo*, created when that Second Treaty of Greenville, or some such, also known as the Pitti Treaty, was redacted and finally enacted and accepted, along with the *Supera Ĉarto*, in that interstitial Interspell Year Lambda.

[The recurrent "Big Tire," "Giant Lake Erie Tire," etc., is perhaps some code for a donut-shaped "universe." In that bastard Nova Esperanto artificial language that is so rapidly spreading and encroaching on English, a konfedo is a "sort of loose confederation," and Supera Ĉarto is roughly "Magna Carta." —Ed.]

This long-buried narrative reaches across harried and strangely prolonged generations, of which I, "D," have been part and flexed with the tide, and it spans what the reader must now know to have been the most chaotic and exciting years in some several millennia, there on the shallow shoals of a new time hole, but to what goal? Not just an entropic and ironic id-seeded greed? No, indeed, as we shall see.

Now drawn together, tardily, from my old journals, tomes, totes, clips, quotes, remembrances, research, correspondence and travel notes—as well as those of the not unbiased Sarah Spiderman Siegfried, with her great activity and political motivity (although, alas for objectivity, as one of the main groovers and movers, she was also a reviser with a proclivity for selectivity in reporting those events of that tense 20th Century, and after)—these mémoires *[sic —Ed.]* have thus been compiled, written, or perhaps even smitten, reforged and disgorged, over several generations and they may go on longer still if, in fact, I don't succeed and complete them or at least bring myself at last in one final act to let them rest and stand at some best point.

So I began this modest transcontinental chronicle as a series of vignettes and silhouettes of some vestiges of the best of my family who (I thought) had long before passed into "Transition," that term used by us rosy Auracrucians of the New Western

Order.

Anyhow, all that vignette business revealed that some of my subjects fit into a grander if somewhat illusory story that I had also longed to write, based on research begun but left undone by Sarah Spiderman Siegfried.

I was to learn that several of these relatives and forebears—including one of my grandfathers—had gone through what I now see as earth-shaking years—a period that Mother and the others spurned and never spoke of in our taciturn family, apparently finding them loathsome and bothersome or beyond their grasp.

And then, there *I* was,
at first a belligerent borderline green-corn virgin,
but born to become submerged
in wilder divergent and worrisome diversions
and finally to know Emil Keldner in a brutal butyl-night
rat cellar,
descend into my own seedy and futile binges
in grainy grecque bathhouse fringes,
ever hiding my own Secret Knowledge,
before finally bursting
and edging towards a solution, in a full-fledged
spiritual evolution.

It is surely my mother's secretiveness about all the family stuff, perhaps especially about my birth—*her* Terrible Secret—that finally drove Dad to rove, then leave, and her to drink and sink into quiet madness and ultimately end it all in what I then called the Nil Delta. The poor, unhappy woman!

An image of the Motherhead in the oven of our Roper-brand gas stove haunts me still, though that is not how she ended, for, when her "Moment of Transition" finally came, she no longer had that stove I recall from childhood, but my memory of her final hour still evokes that sagging old gas appliance, already second-hand and rare in the early Depression years, with its wobbly Queen Anne-style legs, pitted burner grates and ill-fitting oven door, on which in dark cyan on crazed white porcelain was the name R O P E R.

Yes, it was that old Roper oven that she often threatened—jokingly, I thought—to stick her head into, and turn on the gas. The Grim Roper again, you quip? No, just pre-Hip-Age vapors and gin-and-hops capers finally popped and roped *her* in. And, worse, she carried glue and booze in her purse.

So it was because of the role several of these relatives and friends played early in that century and indeed its aftermath that I decided to expand those original sketches I wrote and augment them with my own *mémoires*, as well as some other rougher stuff obtained from the elusive, unreliable, effusive, tough and sometimes truth-abusive Sarah Spiderman Siegfried,

who, incidentally,

had briefly been my tenth-grade English teacher.

From the time my own until-then-outwardly-pale life path crossed anew the rather gothic trail of Sarah one Christmas decades later, the search for the story of these remarkable people was punctuated with a series of coincidences. But then, who indeed has not reflected on his meager existence and marveled at the colliding incidents, the co-events, the comings-together in unstintingly pinching time and relentlessly retrenching place, that the comic twist and clench of the Cosmic Wrench, the Laws of Change, Chance and Chaos cannot account for? In fact, isn't that *What It's All About?*

History, in the sense of Significant Events and Turning Points, is the Divine Accident of Time and Place, I say.

It is as that semblance of human *ac-cid-ens,* in the (Latin) sense of *divine befalling,* if you will, that I view cascading human events and happenings, dragged along behind that vague rogue Chaos, so in-vogue in those entropic days, now finally past.

Who knew?

that the gear spokes were shattered and choked,

the cinch of the linchpin broken,

the whole Wheel congealed,

the Truth concealed in springy chatter,
and the sum of the parts so surreal
that only The Arts could get to the heart of the
stringy quantum batter.
Indeed, it is the Semblance of Accident that both
hides and reveals the Truth, the hidden Divine Purpose,
the Crossing of Paths, the Turning of the Holy Screw,
the Meshing—or Jamming—of the Universal Wormgears....
Oh, fiddle!

I thus attempt to spin a fine line, wrap ten, and combine and entwine apparently diverse forces and eddies, sisal spiral parts and threads, and find that ever-climbing *Green Line* we were assigned to unwind, define and chart out by Professor Whipple in Anthropology 109 so far back, around 1949.

A few observations that may help the reader through all this:
1. Ohio is river country, and even that then-shallow Great Miami River in my native Heventon had beautiful bridges that inspired an etching—my first revelation of Beauty—on those 1930s Official School Tablets of smooth-white paper with fine blue-green rules.
2. The Time Wave whose tidal crest we who can still read are riding into the future is that upward branch of Professor Whipple's once-simple and ample but now ever-thinning and fraying Green Line. Some of us can still conceive of both the synchronic and the diachronic as well as the asynchronous and the isochronous and we have the gift of crib-rail-to-death-knell temporal perception of the Whole Fabric, while those riff-raff masses afflicted with serial dyslexia and the early TV-, VisionSet- and now Netscope-, PodPad-, SensaMask- and CyberStool- induced-and-duped pseudodyslexia only whiffle and waffle and no longer think with linear clarity, missing the weave and warp, and the web-wrap and woven ripple of buried-truffle truth.
3. The Common Denominator is *not* Truth. Given: that if

you take three scrivener's ribbons *[? –Ed.]* and view them as the sides of a triangle, the common denominator is the abstraction of the space enclosed, but the essence is *not* that enclosed space. The signifiers are the lines that define the divine tri-angle. Or is it the "corners," not the lines? The old *Einhalt* vs. *Inhalt.* The turns and forks, not the roads. The uncorked and perhaps even cracked urn, not the wine? The untangled, newfangled, multiforce angeltine angle onslaught. The slant hug o' time.

Those ages ago, when we started this, Sarah and I pronounced: *"This story aims at Truth and, through it, Beauty."*
But we had it backwards, sorta, it turns out.
Fortunately, Truth does not, at least for now, consist of all the facts or acts (as if it ever did), for in the current so-called "Knowledge Base" there is no differentiation between historical fact and spurious "Information."
Blog on!
Better say: *"This story aims at Truth through Beauty."*

As we amble and ramble on in life, we'd better scramble, and gamble on the solemn and sublimely gorgeous shell of that swaggering, ruthless tumble-weave bumble-weed... that ruby booty we've caught anew: Beauty Truth, for, in that lusty Laser Gap final-grasp Last Caper, the ruthless cowboy Cutey Roper, the Prim Greeter Rim-Rasper, the Groping Grab Robber, may well ultimately spare no one who is not a verbal shaper and up to Rapping Rhyme.

Now, later, finally—how far from the end?—after Manhattan was beaten and battened down, maimed and about to be engulfed, we are back in that once glittering Southern California, born again as a leaner and greener Suda Kornukopio and miraculously upheaved to resist the rising seas, with its sprawling city I first

saw at 18, now called Angelus or Angelus Eden,
  and as we rumble along, carrying on
  in Sarah's post-car-age trolley carriage
  (she called it her car cage)
  on the wide and empty ruts of the old auto-routes
  beyond the carrion glut and carnage
  of that earth-rocking age,
  gliding in glee and ragging in mock rage
  and melancholic arsenic gall
  in the once lunatic gray-brown glimmer of that formerly so
gaudy and tawdry "Golden State," now coming alive and green, a
quiet and sublime landscape glowing anew in gleamingly muted
yellow gold, now simple and sublime amid ruins and old shake-
remains,
  we log and gloss those absurd new words
  that now frame the names of the earth-months, the
  measured and metered
  Harfest, Hallow, Hollymount,
  Snowmoon, Frost Thorn, Froth,
  Primtemp, Horn, Fluember,
    and so forth...
  under absinthe sky, then on from gamboge dusk
  through Van Dyck and Pullman-car Brown
  and Drescher's Locomotive Black,
  to pre-dawns of Saponic Sappho Pink, Venus Yellows,
  and Magic Magenta,
  yes, we're on past Dresden, Damask and Baghdad to
  Triage.
  Ah, those newly clear star nights!
  We three. Sarah, C and I.

Chapter 1

Sarah Spiderman Siegfried

Sarah, Miss Spiderman, as I thought of her back in
my tormented and crazed high school days,
was briefly my English teacher and then
mentor until I was in my 20s and entered
a phase of thorny and dazed men-porn days.
Decades later, already ageless, she was to resurface,
re-enter and center my life
and provide some purpose,
assisting in her twisted and firm-fisted
way to fill wormhole gaps
and synoptic cracks in this,
my once-lapsed narrative rap,
but also provide what proved to be mined maps,
set some traps and shoot crap with time perhaps,
all in line with her goal to someway play
a whole host of concomitant controlling
and dominant world roles
hidden from view and known to few.
She was a redhead bred of Saxon stock
blended with threads of Celtic-belt heritage,
despite the German name she carried
(perhaps to be blamed on some surly Teutonic flame
she'd earlier married and possibly buried).
I was a lonely aspiring rhymester, and she was not only

my loving teacher but soon to be a published novelist,
feature story writer and, alas for history,
notoriously unreliable historian.

Her first successes were fiction serials and shorter material
under the signature Sandy Pundit Graveston in *Saturday
Evening Post,* but her novels later appeared as books under
another pseudonym—John Henry Colton as a rule—with a
highly respected publisher, while she was still teaching school.

Her *Sir Hedon* and *Myrrh of Eden,*
were works of fiction
that depicted faded,
sword- and blade-jaded glades
of ruder Crusader decades.

Sarah was thin
and her auburn hair framed
a graceless face
speckled with traces of
microscopic freckles; and
she was very myopic.

None of this of course presaged
Sarah's goal and eventual message
or her role in the ultimate total control
and resultant acts to curb the toll,
carnage and gore of the Oil Wars
and achieve her solution:
the dilution, dissolution,
shredding and shedding
of the whole dead and dreaded
Fe'ral Government, whose failure at wars
and aggression and gore of yore,
bred and led to
our new *Granda Konfedo*
embracing east and west.

[*Nova Esperanto:* Granda Konfedo *is a "Large Loose Confederation."*
As for "fe'ral"(rhymes with Christmas carol) it is uncertain how D or perhaps

Sarah came to reduce "federal" to this annoying form. It may have started as some strange and unnoticed slip of the automatic spell-corrector, but it is more likely a mocking either of one of those Presidents who tended to slur their words, or a crude pun meant to denigrate the federal government itself (not likely, in view of D's generally liberal views and known support for a strong federal government). –Ed.]

    Indeed, I was in love with Miss Spiderman Siegfried,
along with actress Ingrid Bergman,
but these were to be short-lived
objects of confused fires and desires
I'd striven and contrived to invent and fake but
which didn't take hold
and soon boldly expired,
to make way for another phase when
I aimlessly hid my glazed
and still unnamed more hardcore
and unfazed gaze and blazing ache for
oh-so-adored and amazing
Massimo Bastian in the Army Medical Corps.

Sarah finally yielded, left the high school teaching field and went to work at that military air base outside Heventon.

She said she had time to write more novels and fiction in that remote transitional military position after the war. What she never told me, I now realize, is that she also had the chance to promote and cement affections and lance sinister connections with the highly remote, covert and to some extent demented Operations Section that was preparing what was known secretly as Teranet.

That first Teranet was a global grid that used an even now unsurpassed and still secret technology based on a mysterious natural girdle code-named Myrtle Mirth that encircled the earth and was not subject to all the tiring problems that were to befall the much later Internet and World Wide Web and lead to their ensuing skewing and undoing. Sarah's intricate and delicate part in this Teranet start, moreover, cleared the way for her later makeover of fragmentary military communication landlines and her eventual traitorous takeover of those old Internet facilities and satellite utilities.

Years later, after the Internet Trash and Crash, the weird Teranet technology was to be the basis of Sarah's impregnable and private, but not uncorrupted, Alteranet.

Chapter 2

Grandfather George Ludwig Haasen

Dear Sarah,

As you asked, finally here are excerpts from some sketches I wrote awhile back about my maternal grandfather, George Ludwig Haasen (1875-1972?):

One of the earliest stories he recounted was the long-awaited date there in Cairo, Ohio of the 50th wedding anniversary in 1882 of family head Jacob Altsheim, celebrated with a huge spread and the reunion of hundreds of extended family members, to the tune of the Altsheim Family Band up on the grand bandstand. My then seven-year-old grandfather George Ludwig and each of his seven-dozen-plus living cousins got a fifty-dollar goldpiece.

There, buried like a fairy feather, was my grandfather George Ludwig, who bore the ancestral magic light, later set ashore in the pelagic Piscean night.

He was to finish sixth grade in a one-room mixed-age schoolhouse with an outside slosh-loo, dreaming of loon lore and perhaps moon ore, but mostly the Wild West, but he was a good enough scholar and spelling bee winner to be taken on by that printer down the road in Columbus Grove.

"Buffalo Bill" Cody was his hero and, still a lad of barely 18, George went to see Cody's Wild West show at the Chicago

World's Columbian Exposition, that "White City," probably the model for the "Emerald City" of L. Frank Baum's *The Wonderful Wizard of Oz*. There he also rode and reeled on George Washington Ferris's glorious 20-story wheel, became enamored of 19th century industrial marvels and embraced forthwith the myth of the New Century, and all the rest, along with the old, the Wild West.

Then, when the Great Panic of 1893 continued into '94, he went West to join a branch of Jacob Coxey's "Army." He paid his way on the train and went to Oregon to join the ranks of the cocky but hobbled jobless for what was to be perhaps the first "March on the Nation's Capitol," chiefly to promote a Congressional vote for a public works program to relieve the spurned and unemployed mobs.

George joined the odd Coxey contingent to hop the freights bound Back East from the great Far West, and around the campfire one stark coal-dark Iowa night in the unbroken spring cold, he showed off that treasured gold anniversary token to his bizarre mates, hobos and tramps, boot recruits, unemployed stiffs, roustabout blokes, idle woodsmen, cute jocker fundom fruits of ill repute, and the young Jack London.

He boldly passed it around for the admiring but conspiring fold, and, miracle, found he was fleeced of his cherished gold piece. Naive and callow, he'd never feared his bright yellow coin might disappear or be so easily purloined in the hallowed army he'd joined.

> *What else he boldly showed off, doffed, tossed or lost at what*
> *cost, he never told,*
> *but I dream of*
> *the coy demo ploy of a hose dose,*
> *the wry acme-rod sod sword job,*
> *sore cod-bed reams*
> *by a sawyer rod ace run amuck,*
> *and the base doc in the rowdy bawdycar,*
> *an easy-screw crowd, that crew,*

but most of all I seem to summon
a vision of his bucking Woody-Bear!
Boom! beam! cyberdoo Woody-Bear Cowboy Dream.

But one pale-drawn leaden-gray dawn George was gone, for he and That Cowboy curtly deserted these stragglers of Coxey's Army as they at last passed someplace near the Haasen farm in Allen County, while the mob rode the rails on down to Coxey's hometown, Massillon, re-amassed anon and finally moved on, Washington-bound—without my grandfather, although he carried with him through life some of Jacob Coxey's new-found ideas, which were to become the socio-economic element of the Merganser Experimental Work-Shop (MEWS) "Ninety Year Plan to Change the World" that grandfather helped develop.

Even though Grandfather's Woody-Bear Cowboy stayed on, the still-"partly"-pristine aspiring printer and beginning breadwinner was now 22 and he married my grandmother, oh-so-better-be-good Bertha Zoetta Mood, I suppose because he thought he "should."

The newlyweds had been granted a farm by Grandfather Altsheim in return for taking care of one of his daughters, the alarming and ranting, bent and crazy "Aunt Selena," rhymes with hyena. But my naive and still-juvenescent grandmother's reaction to the splinter-brained, loony and senile Selena indirectly ended granddad's planned journeyman printer stint that winter in Columbus Grove.

Indeed, the phantoms of that nutty aunt queen fanned a long series of scenes, and grandmother—she so gleaming clean with Kirk's Coco Castile Hardwater Soap—at a still-lean 19 soon lost hope of caring for the dope, and started to mope.

No, she could not make the grade
or abide the ordeal
and went on the attack and crusaded,
pouted and whimpered
and appealed to George Ludwig to slacken
and back out of the all-but-sealed

surreal-aunt farm deal,
and abandon the bargain, the nutty but harmless old maid,
the charm of the farm, and
his printer trade.
George Ludwig could not dissuade his wife
and indeed faded into a masquerade charade
and bade sad farewell to a bounteous life
in Allen County Ohio,
to his Aunt Selena,
to his beloved sulfurwater
—and to That Woody-Bear Cowboy, I'd guess—
and they moved to Heventon 80 miles south.

Gone forever those farm attics; frantic trunk antics; bulging longjohn yarns. Whew! Wheat dust in the redbarn. Rust. And, uh, oh, ha, the yellow sulfurwater, or black.

In that nest of record hordes of bored descendants of the Altsheims and Haasens, some rough twists, good and bad, developed amidst the interbred genetic stuff, like that sad Aunt Selena. Although these tight-fisted farmers mostly remained pragmatic and static, lispy and asthmatic, with electric refrigerators, shiny cars, large ears and wispy hair, some intertwinings, sporadic sophistication, new tufts and twisted wrinkles in the gray bladder, so to speak, and so on, all coexisted.

Indeed, as the dread Old World trace
of these German immigrants
was shed and all but effaced
and dead in later days,
there was still a shred left,
of somewhat different fleece that reared its head here and there, just as the Pale Rose wound its way through the innermost dregs and drags of the Main River bow that wet spring I spent in Germany in the ancestral backwoods. Secret Knowledge, that trace of magic in the old rhyme of my childhood that I was to see in its ur-form in our ancestral seat at Wildensee:

"Take a piece of wood

"Stick it in the corner
"Take a piece of straw,
"Poke it in the belly
"And out comes a Dutchman,
"Ja, Ja, Ja."
Cattails and pussy willows, witches well, catspring swell; brown-burn bruins' wick. Wheels. Pen wells. Pumps primed. Clanging balls. In damp times everything smells of sulfur. Brine. Pale rose...
... and out comes a Dutchman...
Grandfather considered himself a "Dutchman," as the Germans called themselves there in Allen County, and he had wanted to be a cowboy, like that coy cob-woo guy he had deserted Coxey with, and so loved.

When I began to appreciate him, George Ludwig was escaping into the clarity of an earlier past and it was too late for him to relate what would have been the great story of his meritorious accomplishments. His world was of 1908 draught horses, those scores and scores of still undead first cousins and countless relatives of yore; and he longed to drink sulfur water, yellow or black. Though he didn't even recall the later swirling 1920s, he remembered with furious precision a flurry of events from the turn of that century—
horses crazy and smart, snow and ice, divining rods,
that funeral snafu where the floor fell through,
dead friends, prophetic chicken innards,
plenipotentiary wizards and centenary blizzards—
all this more clear than what had happened
a few minutes before,
or in his fabulous years at the Merganser Experimental Work-Shop.

After the move to Heventon, George Ludwig became a *Bierwagen* driver for his twin cousins, the foolish and *schwuhl* Schwantz Brewery brothers, but as he often came home smelling of beer, ever-fretting Bertha Zoetta would get in a snit, yell and throw a fit, and finally she compelled him to quit. He forthwith apprenticed to the Drescher Brothers, Hermann and Heinrich, clannish old Rhineland varnishmakers, who hired him because he could speak a German dialect and print neat paint and varnish can labels in English.

Until his very end he talked of rail carloads and tubs of exotic substances from the forlorn far bourns and corners of the earth, Around the Horn—lampblack, cinnabar, dragon's blood, vermilion, turpentine, terps, resin, rosin.

Ah, the resin taste of retsina wine—all we could find—those Athens nights, and the hairy knees of that guy, from Oklahoma... unnoticed by FiFi MacP.

Or Poe's Amontillado, vino so naively sought, in vain, before settling for other booze, there in Veracruz. And weeks later by train to Nogales, my face covered with soot from the engine, or was it? That same epic July day of the Trinity Atomic Test not far away!

Come alive in '45!

The same seething cloud Grandfather saw foaming in a magic wormhole? The Haasen slot? A lower ohm? Morel mushroom whorl? Boo! A new omphalos burned in the earth.

Poke it in the belly,

out comes...

Sadly, until it was too late, George Ludwig seemed to me only a slightly gruff and rough, rubescent, goofy but arduous yokel rube. And I thought his only escape from soul-scraping scream-scape bedroom boredom came from those cowboy dreams.

We thundered 80 miles north from Heventon what seemed a hundred times in fumy old cars, along that brick road, the Dixie Highway I so hated, to spend terrible Depression weekends in the kin country, past furrowed fields and rural boroughs: Troy, Piqua (where you picked your way), Sidney, and Wapakoneta (Wapak). Anna, then Botkins—or was it the other way around?—a highway long since lopped off the main route, now broken gaps, lapsed and passed off the maps.

And finally Lima, rhymes-with-Aunt-Jemima, would greet us with that locomotive plant and a smelly refinery's slimy slue along the defeated, slow and clogged Hog Creek, officially logged as the Ottowa River.

Then on to Cairo and a little beyond, and finally delivered unharmed to the haven of Aunt Till and Aunt Bess's farm, a forty-acre homestead stake past the Lincoln Highway, after the little graveyard.

Trains across the flat fields.

The first thing George Ludwig did when he arrived in Allen County was tromp across the damp wood back-porch floor to the pump and gulp down two good tincups of the yellow-brown sulfurwater.

Sulfur water comes in two varieties, yellow and black. Various sulfide and sulfate compound lumps actually float in it, swirling about in the tincup after it is hand-pumped from the well. Hydrogen sulfide gas is of a flammable class and alas when passed can be poisonous and poison us in high concentrations. When hydrogen sulfide is introduced to water, let us be quick to chide, a not-soon-forgotten "rotten egg" taste and smell may result and not subside. —Vidi-World Web

That sets the backstage, heh?

Sorry this is a bit of a jumble, dearest Sarah, but it's from the heart.

Yours,

D

Chapter 3

My Other Grandfather

Dear Sarah:

Okay, here's about the only thing I can remember concerning my paternal grandfather, Vincent Madison Hamilton, except that there was a tea cart in his living room.

In one of the few tête-à-têtes
I was ever to get with Grandfather Hamilton,
with some acerbity
he showed me an empty whiskey flask
he had in storage of obvious antique
origin, vintage and mintage.
He told me it had held the dregs
of the only booze
that had ever been used
under his roof,
and that he had been enticed
on the advice and begging
of community pillar Dr. Dillard Miller
to buy it; and that he'd bought it
and brought it
home to save the ebbing life
of his ailing wife Ebelazeth,
who was already failing and
lying there on the brink of death,
dying of flu that spring.

But she would only shrink
from the liquor,
could not drink it,
and quickly grew sicker and sicker
and departed this mean life and scene.
    Affectionately,
           D

And from Sarah I got:

Dearest D:
After Ebela was gone
your Grandfather Hamilton found
the booze was gone too and he was drawn
to believe that the vile drink
had been drunk
by a crass red-headed housekeeper lass
he'd hired early that year before Ebelazeth passed,
a convert he had searched out
in the Sacred Arbiter Presbyterian Church,
but this brave Hannah Maeve Jesterson
was of low-class and given to sass
and even blasphemy, he protested.
Then after his Ebelazeth breathed her last
he would have fired and
retired Hannah on grounds
that he had found
she might have ingested a few drops
of that schnaps,
but, alas, the wild lady
was no longer girthed tight and
was fat with child.
Yes, this jolly dolly
was soon to give birth
behind the scenes

to a son,
on January First, 1919.
Although old Vincent was a settled teetotaler,
a man of convincing conviction,
and a deacon of fine diction
speaking in the service of his church,
and though freely given to quarrel with
the pathetic morals and ethics
of those within his jurisdiction,
he had an addicting affliction himself,
a dereliction, I perceive and believe,
that had led him for fun
to the redhead's bed
and bred her that son...
that effervescent Other One,
our own hero, Thom Jesterson.
                              —Sar

Dear Sarah—

Your conjecture that my grandfather might have been Thom Jesterson's father seems absurd and out-of-character, and your raising the question only leads me to wonder about the other information you have supplied. My father was as silent as my mother concerning the events of the 1920s. He was but 17 when his mother died, and he claims he has no recollection of the Irish Hannah you mention. But on further reflection, I suspect it may well have been my own father who did this deed, thus making Thom my half-brother!

Yours in confusion,

d

Chapter 4

The Mergansers and Thom Jesterson

So, it is only these many years later, with the help of Sarah, that I have been able to piece together missing details of my two grandfathers' lives: the covert participation by one in the Merganser Experimental Work-Shop, known as the MEWS, and what was eventually naively named the "Ninety Year Plan to Change the World"; and the notion that my other grandfather (or perhaps more likely my father) may have sired that so-important Thom Jesterson, who was to be adopted by Ideth and Wem Merganser. Sarah claims that young Thom came to be adopted by the Mergansers through the intermediary of my Great-grandmother Mary Wrenn, who apparently took Thom's Irish mother in during the latter stages of her pregnancy, though Sarah has never documented this.

I had no idea what the MEWS was, although, by coincidence I had met Merganser's wife, Ideth Besuch. And I had caught a glimpse on several occasions and been strangely and strongly attracted to someone I now realize was the Mergansers' adopted son Thom, possibly my half-brother, or that of my father.

Much of what I've learned about the Mergansers comes from Sarah, though I doubt that all of it is accurate. Here's Sarah's report, in her own weird style:

Dearest D,
The night of Merganser's death, Ideth Besuch Merganser took her

promising and precocious foster son, Thomas Jesterson, into the great
expanse of her carved walnut bed in the early-Victorian Main Street
mansion in downtown Heventon with its antimacassar auntie-scarves
and frayed-thread stair-tread—to comfort him, she said.
　　Ideth cupped Thom's ear into a cone and whispered through
the crisp night.
He listened quietly and intently
as she intermittently sipped glistening
warm and slightly silver
curdled goat milk and laid out a cascade
of ambitious plans for the
precocious young blade of a man.
His ear was tickled, scratched and blistered
by the perilous short-cropped bristles
above the purple ripple tip
of the upper lip of this otherwise quite
fine-mien but not-so-feminine Ideth,
and when he tried to giggle she clasped her small still-fleshy
hand across his fresh mouth and nose and tooth-sucked on his
ear a long minute until a riveting shiver rose vise-like in the
mesh of his unshrouded thrill-river, cascading through his
breathless maturing body, ending in a massive spasm
in the lower demon-dome chasm
of his abdomen,
with a fiery burn in the funnel
of the umbilicus tunnel,
that numb infundibulum,
blind and dumb fun-lid
there above
the venal fur-bedecked unnamable lower domain,
as the brush of her rough cheek and tough jaw grazed and
excited his fresh young flesh.
She then again and again pressed with her palms against the
sleek zones of his prominent facial bones, where there was a
paltry bit of stiffening fuzz that he saved next to the places he

already shaved, if somewhat prematurely,
pure myrtle tones,
that erotic thrill-lint,
through and through
that tore to the wave core
when he shaved,
such that he craved
the blade at least once a day.
And now near full-blown,
and thorny-horned,
he was filled with
a rhetoric lilting trill
and a torch-like light-rite chorus,
that licked the hot-tic itch and
trolled his thrill-rill to the hilt.

That was a long and unfulfilling night, but the brave soldierboy
survived the grisly girdle-yeast fate, and next morning at bleak daybreak
he childishly played with an antique gilded horse-and-hearse toy, for his
foster father Wem Merganser, had died the day before, they said.

Ideth had inherited a small paper mill in Heventon, which grew
rapidly and became Merganser Paper Products. The company proved to
be one of the more viable of the giant Heventon industrial enterprises,
even though it was not one of those solemnly reliable and venerable
giants created back in the previous century. Unlike so many of the great
Heventon companies that sank in the financial quagmire of '29, this
conglomerate empire that included a small newspaper chain was not
destined to expire in that fiscal unwinding, and in fact it thrived. So
Wem's demise was not among those suicides that grew out of shame and
corrupt failure those bleak October days.

Enlightened industrial genius, arid and unsung patriarch to his
workers—though hardly paterfamilias—Merganser, in one version,
had been found the day before hanged—or at least dangling—from a
tree in the Western Meadows, a rear portion of the Merganser Estate.

Another story I have unearthed is that he had had himself frozen at the MEWS in some early cryogenic experiment. But I tend to believe that he was still alive and had merely gone into seclusion someplace, not "Transition."

There were dual ceremonies. The public funeral was presided over by the Reverend Al Gonquin at the Sacred Arbiter Presbyterian Church, there in downtown Heventon. The employees of the mill had been given the day off to file past the closed and perhaps empty casket, as the terrapin-like minister looked on.

The funeral procession to the burial site was eerie because the five Merganser company cars carried only the wives of board members, for, at the same hour as the baleful finale of the public funeral, most of the remaining members of Heventon's brute industrial elite were seated behind the elegant doors of the 14th-floor Beaux Arts boardroom of the Spring National Bank.

Here, old Jonathan Spring the Second allowed the prematurely pubescent Thom Jesterson—face flushed and bright or perhaps still eroded red from the questionable delights and rites (and perhaps slight bites) of his sleepless night in Ideth's ready bed—to sadly but brashly cast Merganser's purported ashes out the window.

Yours from the heart,
  Sar

Dear Sar (as you recently signed)—
  Where did you get all that weird stuff about Thom J. in Ideth's bed and Merganser's perhaps feigned death? I really find it hard to believe. And, wasn't "the early-Victorian Main Street mansion in downtown Heventon" you imagine with "antimacassars" and "frayed stair-treads" torn down in 1922 after the new Merganser estate was completed? Also, as you say, Merganser was hanging from a tree in the "Western Meadows" on the rear of the estate— hardly likely in Downtown Heventon!
  Incredulously but ever assiduously,
    d

Be that all as it well may, some of the more prurient parts

of Sarah's tale may have been untruthful products of her fruitful imagination and fascination with fresh and sleek pubescent masculine cheeks and passion for ephebic Greek physiques, urgently burgeoning beard and the hopefully concomitant allure of pure and immature but stirring emerging growth of efflorescent male body down, the even sheath of cherished chest hair, and so on, not to mention male pectoral budding. (I was fifteen when she was my English teacher.)

I've learned that Wem was generally known simply as Merganser, while his wife was most often called by her full maiden name, Ideth Besuch, or, oddly enough, "Miss Besuch."

We don't know how the two met, though Ideth may well have been a certain younger figure of androgynous nature who was said to accompany Wem around Manhattan in the 1890s. Although the earliest mentions in Heventon newspapers allude to them as a couple, they were apparently never seen together and the only photos are of one or the other, not both.

In any case, here's what I've found and believe to be true:

Merganser was born in Heidelberg, Germany in 1871, perhaps of French and German parents. In my own family archives I've discovered that he may have actually been a distant cousin of my grandfather George Ludwig, and an earlier Merganser probably fought with a great-uncle of my grandfather at the Battle of Jena under Napoleon in 1806. Both had been conscripted into the Napoleonic army and later deserted, settling in the Odenwald, where both families had their roots.

In 1871—that year of disorder, rifts and war, swift drift and then peace with reordered and shifted borders for those squabblers over the Rhine—the little Wem was abandoned to foster parents, then bundled off to Grenoble, through unknown circumstances.

We next hear of him in New York around 1888.

From what Sarah has told me, it appears that Wem was indeed an orphan, and by the late 1880s he led a life that paralleled the likes of certain super-hyped Horatio Alger types.

Sarah says that what she calls (in one of her many obscure and imperfect anagrams) her "error-chase" (research) has him in his earliest teens a lean pimp (!) of sorts spasmodically in the New York City scene, but knowing her, let me assure the reader that this could well be her own mad fantasy. She attests that he appeared "successful" and doubtless dressed well, catering his "charges" largely to the best well-to-do clients, whom he once said he viewed as "stepping stones to the very rich."

He was seen regularly, Sarah says, often with a handsome, even younger, well-honed but small-boned young man *[Ideth? – Ed.]* in tow, and the two were fixtures in "quirky beau-monde literary coteries and refined and high-toned artistic circles, such as they were in the Gotham of the late 1880s. He went to museums and ventured into rare, select and esoteric cultural lectures in his spare time and quickly earned the reputation of being a neat and effete teenage arts patron, tart-pursuer and rant-pastor pant-raster parson star," Sarah has dared to write, which makes absolutely no sense to me. "It was generally thought he was the son or scion of some better-known big figure. He may have looked four or five years older than he was, this cock-sure and paradoxical mockery of the flock and stock of bedrock Gotham gentry."

Wem and Ideth apparently moved to Heventon after she inherited the paper mill around 1898. The disappointing fact is that we seem to have more "information"—true or not—about him in the 19th century than during the important 1920s period, when he apparently sought public obscurity and was nothing like the colorful blade of his amazing earlier days that Sarah described.

Some of Sarah's possible fabrications may also perhaps be explained as attempts to live out her own derelictions, fictions, confections and predilections, and create a universe to her compulsive specifications in a sort of massive revision and personal collusive world-encompassing version of history to fulfill her predictions.

And at times I think she may have viewed or construed what she accomplished, or provoked, as one big many-hued practical joke. I think for her Truth was diaphanous and her crafty role was to dig it out and see through it, then dress it up and control it, but not extol it.

Despite what may have been his strange beginning, Merganser seems to have ended up an honest and generous man, fair and perhaps even devout. And he undoubtedly made a significant but quiet and generally unrecognized contribution to the MEWS he founded.

I have learned that he was active in the local lodge of the Knights of Pythias, where he met my grandfather George Ludwig, who was the lodgemaster. The two embraced that fraternal organization's "egalitarian humanitarian" principles, and these were to inspire the Merganser Experimental Work-Shop and its Damon-and-Pythias camaraderie, as well as many of the goals the Work-Shop researchers aspired to reach, including what they hoped would be a new world peace. But Merganser also hoped to develop a "new kind of Universal Substance" with modifiable properties that would serve many purposes.

The idea for the Work-Shop seems to have blossomed before 1920, and by 1921 my grandfather had taken a leave from the varnish factory and was working with Merganser.

Chapter 5

Ideth Besuch

Ideth was not among those industrial bores reported to have assembled in the Spring National Bank 14th floor boardroom during Wem Merganser's funeral. Although the rumor was bruited about that she had collapsed and was sequestered in the apse of the stanchioned Merganser mansion, in effect, she was driven 200 miles from there early on the funeral morning in a stately European limousine, perhaps of Spanish mark, and delivered to Marietta, on the Ohio River in the southeastern part of the state, where the massive machine parked in front of the already ancient Flying Cloud Hotel on Front Street.

She would spend the next afternoon there in the shabby but private old Foc's'l Room off the lobby with Otto Tafteh, a mystic and foxy Turkish carpet merchant, who had earlier claimed to be the owner of Blennerhassett Island in the Ohio River a few miles downstream from Marietta.

It was during this meeting that Ideth had planned to purchase that island, which was known primarily for its original owner Harman Blennerhassett's support of what came to be known as the Burr Conspiracy, widely thought to be a plot by Aaron Burr around 1805 to take over Spanish-held territories and form a new country.

Although drawn to Blennerhassett Island because of its historical significance, Ideth was apparently unfazed when it proved to be the *village* of *New* Blennerhassett that Otto actually offered to sell her and which she agreed to buy, not the island. New Blennerhassett was a tiny settlement nudged into a remote gully a few miles from the Ohio River that had once been pillaged by local Indians and left vacant. She managed to find the plans for the old Blennerhassett mansion, which had burned to the ground in the early 19th century anyway, and had a replica built at New Blennerhassett, where she created a sort of island by diverting the nearby creek into a wide moat that was dug around the new compound. Although this was to be Ideth's secret retreat, it was not until more than a score of years later that, in partnership with Sarah, she moved the political branch of the MEWS there.

The actual execution of the 1930s Ninety Year Plan had been further engineered in fleeting but heated 1940s meetings in the backroom of the string of newspapers Ideth published, where Sarah Spiderman Siegfried had become an editor, then finally perfected at New Blennerhassett by her and Sarah through decades of stingy springs sown stone-gray with wet Ohio snow, and so on. Here they eventually hatched assorted new contorted schemes and dreams that aspired to get what was to be the Thom Jesterson Trio embedded to rewire Washington and conspire to bring out of that Fe'ral mire the new *Granda Konfedo.*

Otto referred to himself as a "latter-day Aaron Burr," and his secessionist ideas, though not entirely in concert with those of Ideth and later Sarah, emulated those of that Federalist Vice President and duelist Aaron Burr. *[In the spring of 1805, Burr set off down the Ohio River from Pittsburgh in a specially-prepared boat he called his "ark," eventually reaching Blennerhassett's Island, a 300-acre piece of land in the river just downstream from Parkersburg and Marietta. The island's owner, Harman Blennerhassett, invited Burr to dinner, and Burr's "conspiracy" was discussed, though it has never been determined with any certitude what his plans were. Blennerhassett pledged his support, and was eventually charged with treason along with Burr, but they and others were never convicted. –Ed.]*

Otto's son, known as Jack Taffeta, who was to become a member of the Jesterson Trio, was rumored to have been the clandestinely-born child of Ideth and he apparently grew up somewhat isolated at New Blennerhassett.

At the New Blennerhassett MEWS, Ideth and Sarah also planned the inscrutably- and confusingly-named New Mews-Manhattan Emerald Gardens Project, *[Although we seem to remember mews is an old English term referring to a row of townhouses with stables, available resources will not confirm this. –Ed.]* to be built in the truncated 21st Century. Later, they would develop other more secret "island" compounds: on the man-made St. Nola in the below-sea-level salty Slanto Sea in Suda Kornukopio, and another in Nomo Lake in the *Alta Nevada Siero* (High Sierras). Finally, Sarah would establish the now totally destroyed Scientific Institute for the Study of Time (SIFTSOFT) hidden away in the mountains above Burndale, near Angelus Eden (formerly Los Angeles), which turned out to be, perhaps not coincidentally, at the epicenter of that recent Terrible Temblor.

Sarah said little of Ideth Besuch's origin, except that her father had been a colleague and disciple of Dr. Robert Green Lingersoul, that great archetypal 19th century American agnostic and mystic.

Ideth was a friend of the cruel, domineering but spiritual Louie Meershelrook, for whom I worked as a subservient, obedient and psychologically abused but less than fervent teenage household servant during my high school years. Louie told me again and again that it was while she herself was visiting one of the enthralling agnostic Lingersoul summer "camps" one fall in the 1890s at Finger Lakes, New York, north of Dresden and Burnham Point, that she had her first "spiritual initiation" by a "giant bird-like beast that came in out of the East and shat" *[sat? –Ed.]* on her bed.

Variations of this neat and convenient if incomplete and fleeting apparition were to repeat throughout her life and continue to evolve, including one incident when the beast dissolved and resolved into a Jesus vision that Louie told me emerged from her downstairs "water closet" there on Salem Avenue in Heventon around 1936, thanked her for letting him "use the faucet" and "take a light" and, right before her in the gloomy shade of her faded kitchen, urged the old tyrant to take what she called an "airship" to California. She says he directed her to California to meet Sister Sarah Louise Haasen near Hemet, who, I've recently surmised, was the daughter of Grandfather George Ludwig's brother Will, the first mayor of the Los Angeles suburb Burndale. Sister Sarah Louise was a minister of a fundamentalist church in Hemet she had founded that proved to be greatly at odds with the more esoteric Lingersoul teachings. Louie returned to Heventon, angry and disillusioned.

Chapter 6

The Merganser Estate

My recollection of my only visit to the Merganser Estate, when I was in high school, is extremely vague, so I rely on an old typescript, filled with fantasies, from the late 1940s—done long before I ever considered doing the present account.

Of course I had no notion then that there were any, much less many, connections between the Mergansers and my grandfathers.

I leave the old typescript intact, more or less.

The Merganser estate was in a southern suburb of Heventon, obscured and smothered by a fence of dense brambles. Behind it lay a sort of laboratory in a huge old English mill I've heard referred to as the MEWS.

The house itself was a rambling half-timbered mansion, perhaps built in the early 1920s. I went there with my high school friend, fur-pawed Felix, to repair a grandfather clock, for we were antique clock experts and fixers in our high school days.

When Felix and I went to the Merganser estate, Ideth Besuch had long been head of the Merganser paper empire, in fact and action since the wreath of grief for her husband hung on the hearth.

Still svelte, Merganser's widow, known to us as "Miss Besuch," ran her own household as well as the Merganser industrial empire and a string of conservative newspapers that included the Heventon Times, and it was with her that we dealt, Felix and I, the odd teen "clockboys" pair, for the grandfather clock affair.

Ideth Merganser was a small, vaguely masculine, stork-like lady whose head and neck projected forward, and her stern matriarchal back was neither arched nor stooped. She carried a knurled cane in a starkly patrician *[?–Ed.]* manner. Her hair was now lavender-white, her pleated blouse crisp and precision-starched. She had all the marks of one who had led and acted, lived and loved, fought and fugued *[?–Ed.]* and grown into a raw and ragged gnarly old war dog, it seemed to me.

When Felix and I were there working on the hickory case clock, I saw for the first time the hard flash and fascinating cock-walk of the dashingly handsome red-locked foster son flit quickly through the broad tapestried corridor. What struck me most was not only his rubicund coiffe but also the lush rufescent growth of hair on his hands and protruding from his stiff white shirt, with a snippet of erect and rough embroidered priapus-shaped flowers and puffed sleeves with ruffled cuffs in a "peasant" style I had never seen before. This same charismatic figure was to appear in the background of a photo the Heventon Times published of me with some congressman or other at an Antioch College International Peace Conference a year later, along with Wilmar Scheedick, whom I had actually met at an Auracrucian rite.

He smiled an urgent smile on slightly turgid lips, seemed on the verge of standing watch firmly in the corridor for a minute or more, then left, stopped in his tracks, turned back, nodded, burned, and so on. On the third pass he came in, said hello, and then seemed to disappear. I was never to forget the brotherly stirrings this striking hirsutorufous being aroused in my clean,

still somewhat pristine body and green, naive and
unrefined mind.

Disappeared? Dickery-dock into a secret
corridor (rod rise correct, sire!) behind an oak
panel--an okay for a penny poke or penial peek?--
through to a stairway to the mansard rooms for a
slam-ram in the sand with randy grooms and Moors?
[? –Ed.]

But how could I know? In denial, did I go?

Faint perfumes of Immortelle, Impatiens,
Inconnu, Indian Mallow, Inkberry, St. Andrews
Cross and Jewelweed. A fish among fowlers;
find one. O, luxuriant locks! Fulgurant bulge
divulging the presently erupting rod pod.

That corridor is ever there in my mind. The
ruby glow of red filoplumes caught in a shaft of
dusty light.

Though I did not then know his name, this phantom I now
know as Thom, had perhaps always been in my dreams and
would be forever. A fantasy, like that fleeting bad lad ever across
the street, never had; a lost brother?

Chapter 7
Wilmar Scheedick

Wilmar Scheedick, destined to be one of the principals in the MEWS, though Thom Jesterson never was, had spent the first of his clearly austere early and routinely innocent years in the funky "Hunkytown" area of North Heventon. Born in 1914 and soon to be orphaned, he was already a very mature adolescent in the late '20s, and a very comely young man when I met him in the early '40s at a somewhat laconic and tangled white rite I'd gone to out of curiosity, to watch the Auracrucians mark the vernal equinox in Triangle Park.

Was *he* to be the brother I longed for? I was a lad of 14 and he was handsome and lean, though his features were a little too prominent, his libertine mouth a bit rent and nose slightly bent to one side, and he had a thick whack of coal-black hair. A really beau hunk, a "Hunky" or "Bohunk," (from "Bohemian Hung Arian") [probably "Bohemian Hungarian" –Ed.]

In Heventon, the term "Hunky" was not-so-slyly applied to almost any earnest Eastern European
steerage Crimean, Aegean peon,
plucky and spunky flunky
immigrant grunt or descendant thereof.

In 1921, through my great-grandmother, Mary Wrenn (who had also arranged the adoption by the Mergansers of the illegitimate Thom Jesterson), seven-year-old Wilmar H.

Scheedick was to arrive with great aplomb one winter gloaming at the Merganser's home as an older gloomy "playmate" for Thom Jesterson.

Although Wilmar had great drive, and strived and contrived to thrive and survive, and was treated in many ways as an equal of Thom, he was not to become a sibling sequel, for no formal agreement was ever completed and the Mergansers discreetly opted not to adopt him, as they had Thom, so Wilmar always resided and slept in the servant part of the house, except when he fervently crept, unintercepted, into Thom's bed at night yearning to quell what he called "The Burn."

Redheaded Thom was talented, artistic, ferociously precocious, lively, outgoing and both active and attractive, while Wilmar, perhaps belying his gypsy origins, was dark, moody, mysterious, cloudily broody and given to saying surprising cryptic and apocalyptic things. He had occasional loquacious, even salacious outbursts of what some called "talk-fits," perhaps a mild form of Tourette's syndrome, and he sometimes audaciously walked about the spacious home with what might have been an imaginary violin tucked under his chin, chanting, "I am Anton, Anton, the ma-gypsy-man of the gypsy-men."

Anguished agrarian Hungarians had been brought in great numbers into factory-rimmed northeast Heventon at the turn of the old century and one large contingent had been "imported" by a labor contractor to work in a railroad car factory and forced to live in a coarse and appalling compound, surrounded by an offensive 12-foot fence.

The Hunkies made nine dollars for 72 hours work a
week and lived in this weedy enclave in cramped houses.
They purchased their needs
at the premises store
with base brass tokens
crassly issued on payday
and if they broke the cruel rule

and bought elsewhere, they'd surely be sacked.

This bastion of agony, a company town called the Kossuth Colony, had by far the largest bar in that gritty margin of the city.

But during the awful Heventon Flood of 1913,
the tall wooden walls were all torn down
and the timbers were banded together
to craft rescue boats and rafts
to float out the people stranded downtown,
carry them off in the mud and blood,
and land them safe on higher ground.
But the offending fence
was never rebuilt,
perhaps out of guilt.

So, by the time Wilmar was born, at least the awful wall was all gone.

Wilmar's mother was a gypsy and she and her husband Anton had craftily contrived to keep their lives together, come hell or wry weather, and work in the same place, she polishing superior wood grain in the train car interiors.

She sometimes intoned a soft riff of Gypsy tunes, told fortunes and was credited with flowering psychic powers, though she hardly understood the occasional confusing and pseudo-erudite often-English words she chanted in her rants, such as one Wilmar quoted in a letter of his I've treasured:

"Sometimes, to avoid light, the dark carriage drove among the groves, returning each afternoon, every letter the same. The same color and the same general appearance, for it is a true story. Then, black Carrion narcosis..." etc.

One day the image perhaps presaged in that message came to life—and death—as a dread rail carriage, a red caboose, shifted and ran loose in the rail-car yard, escaping silently from the blockage, as it coasted quietly down upon the loving couple to reek swift ravaging havoc and horrible carnage.

Wilmar was subsequently cared for by Imre Karuso who was a type designer at the Manmark Marking Machine factory. He delivered the young lad each morning to a Franklin Elementary School kindergarten class with the same teacher I was to have years later, and the boy spent the afternoons nearby with my Great-grandmother Wrenn, who was to arrange for his later care by the Mergansers, as I said.

When I met Wilmar at that Auracrucian equinox rite, he told me he had worked "in an experimental laboratory" since he was 16, when he may have left the Merganser household for a time, become active in the Auracrucian Order and lived at least part-time in a room he rented on Xenia Avenue. The name Xenia fascinated him, a word having to do with being a stranger, result of hybrid crossing, etc. As an Auracrucian he said he had taken the name Pyro*xene* (mine is Pensator), because he suffered from "The Burn,"

an umbilical-depravity U-burn

cavity problem probably related to gravity.

The mineral pyroxene, he told me, was "said to be a foreign substance when found in igneous rocks; hence its name, which means 'stranger to fire'." He thought that evoking the coldness, the deadness of the anomalous mineral would be his cooling salvation.

I, as well, have this U-burn bane, and boon.

A stranger to the world, he gave gifts to strangers. "Take this xenium from me," I think he intoned, waving his hand in the air after our meeting in the 1940s, as well as in three later oddly scrawled letters I could hardly read. Or was it genius, geranium? gisium?

And, indeed, he told me in the last of his letters that he was about to go on what he called a "distant voyage to a strange isle," and I never knew whether this was a spiritual or an actual physical trip.

I thought I would never see him again, but then, several

years later he reappeared at that International Peace Conference I attended at Antioch College, real violin and all, and said he then lived on a "far isle." I realized much later that might be the fake island New Blennerhassett.

Chapter 8

Man Draake

Fragments

[These fragments are retained because they were apparently notes for the section of this chapter that follows. They both shed light on and raise some questions concerning the subsequent material as well as the previous chapter. —Ed.]

The Indian poet
Ravin Erostag
sired a manchild
Emmanuel Draake (rhymes with rake)
Phyphe Sysyphus bird seed
of Cosmic Conception.
Sister Mother "Aunt" Idasora.
Powder-baked in some sort of Calumet amulet without
testicular ejaculate?
An Arm-and-Hammer soda-faking ode to forsaken-photos,
a descendant of the Armory L'escalier and amour harmony?
Nude Dá-dà dude Papa Marcel's douche-hay lay,
our sleazy Champs-'e-lazy lady?
The three to the Meershelrook episode,
which was so traumatic...
boyish gypsy quality youth
that (s)he had carried
survived the Work-Shop and

more than one terrible experiment
a lover, Wilmar
a farm northeast
Sibelius Violin C…
Antioch letter
away to a "distant island"
"Little wonder" that Generations later,
I connect him with a "similar disappearance."
A man.
A callow and sinuous curly hair
sandy
"…girls?" (in the manner of the old days)
"Dating?" he asks.
Tingles, strange menses [sic. –Ed.]
through my limbs,
for I never in high school,
except under the most traumatic circumstance,
the talk of my hairy teenage high school mates.
Hellzapoppin'
Man Draake
in the mechanical aspects
though not the chemistry,
his life work, artificial insemination,
a number of unusual surgical practices,
the magnetic "center" and
the Ergon, "pure energy, the properties, both matter and energy."
Rational, mechanical Nature
his resolution Universe,
his "findings" in the turn of thought.
Lives that were truly fantastic and wove a fabric,
a "triage" in several senses, a harvest,
a cutting, that spread across three or four states
of mind for decades, perhaps centuries,
foreshadowed by genetic advances.…
And George Ludwig's belief in resin.

The bulbar rat, a bubonic Bulgar bougie bugger,
the Blue Parrot Bar on Santa Monica Boulevard...
the few accounts I have been able to reconstruct from the
family history place it in Pittsburgh in the middle of
the afternoon.
[Pittsburgh occurs several times in the correspondence and elsewhere. It is no
doubt some kind of code word D and Sarah used. The fragment ends here. —Ed.]

Emmanuel Draake

Dear Cookie,

I suppose you know the kids' nickname for you at Farview High School was "Cookie."

You've asked about my recollections of Louie Meershelrook and Man Draake.

You'll recall that when I was so close to you in my adolescent years I was working for Louie. This was a very traumatic time for me, and I have never been able to write or even think very directly about it. But I do remember clearly an autographed deep-sepia photo Louie had of that earliest precursor of modern dance, Idasora Phyphe Nutcan, and some things she told me about Idasora's sister and the great Indian poet (Ravin) Erostag, he of such polymath radiance and girth on the holy bubble path. Louie said she had known both Idasora and Erostag and that Erostag had had a child, Emmanuel, in 1901 with Phoebe Draake, an obscure, if not totally unknown woman who claimed, perhaps without basis, to be a sister of Idasora.

I know you believe this Erostag provenance of Emmanuel was a myth, but I really much prefer this version. And I found quite a bit of supporting information, to wit:

The wild and beguiling macho-lad issue of this union between Phoebe and Erostag was referred to as "Mon Petit Dragon" in certain notes I found in Louie's home there on Salem Avenue after her 1947 death, on the back of that framed photo on the stair landing.

Though he was apparently named Emmanuel Draake, some called him Mandragon, Mondragon or Man Draake, and I've found he was referred to as a "manchild," perhaps because of his wild precocity. Although samples found recently at the MEWS of sperm and blood provide mild DNA evidence of the Erostag stud-worm paternity, and though the odd pair of Erostag and Phoebe does seem to have produced this heir, there seems to be little evidence that the two ever had an enduring affaire. *[Although DNA was described as early as the 1930s, its use for tracing parentage came much later, which renders this sentence totally suspect; it could not have been in the original of this old letter to Sarah. –Ed.]*

Idasora Phyphe Nutcan and Phoebe were known to refer to Emmanuel (perhaps facetiously?) as having arisen out of "an immaculate perception." *[sic –Ed.]*

Emmanuel grew up in the most outrageous of circumstances and exciting of times as part of the entourage of that gallant and talented dancer who gallivanted throughout much of the world. His somewhat unraveled mother Phoebe drifted about with his "Aunt" Idasora, but Phoebe was certainly not as smart or gifted in the arts as was the brisker and friskier Idasora.

After Idasora's two children died in that bizarre Hispano-Suiza scarf incident on the wharf in 1913, *[D has apparently confused this disastrous event with a much later catastrophe that befell a later dancer. –Ed.]* Idasora cast off "Mon Petit Dragon," as she had come to call her progeny, and he was sent to live in Heventon in an attic room of the sort of foster home for unwanted children run by my Great-aunt Hattie Hamilton Druderie, sister of my grandfather Vincent Madison Hamilton.

Man Draake was aware early in life of the whispered mysteries of his own perhaps exceptional conception, and he synthesized the versions of it he heard and fantasized various "perversions," such as a procedure known as "artificial insemination," in those days when such unperfected procedures in humans were thought scandalous.

In the remote attic corner of fanatical Aunt Hattie's rambling old house on wood-block-paved Oxford Avenue just off Salem in Heventon, the young Emmanuel kept pigeons and was ecstatic to be able to devote himself briefly but in earnest to the fruitful pursuits which were to occupy and affect much of his life— the study of the mechanical aspects of reproduction, practical and beneficial methods of artificial insemination, development of a number of unusual surgical as well as somewhat magical procedures involving the omphalos, which he called the magnetic "center" of the human body, and refinement and realignment of his concepts of that "fiery titanic iceberg of urge," the mysterious and ill-defined Ergon, "that tiniest tightly wound spring-like spiral particle" he theorized had the "manner, properties and liberties of both matter and energy."

By the time I was able to question Aunt Hattie about all this, her memory, though quite precise about the past in general, was oddly confused about the strange Emmanuel Draake.

Dark-mane Man Draake was soon to be put in touch with Merganser, for, to settle an old debt of sorts to Aunt Hattie's rude brother, my grandfather Hamilton, Merganser agreed to take Man on at his newly established Experimental Work-Shop, the MEWS, in 1921, thus ridding Hattie of the bizarre youngster.

And under Man Draake's Ring Theory, which he later called the Spiral Spring Theory, developed at the MEWS, heavy concentrations of what he defined as Ergon, that matter-energy-thing, were to be found, he suggested, in the omphalos, which may be what renders it so magnetic, or vice versa *[? –Ed.]*, there where lay the magic net of gentle silken mica agents, the ilk of a minced lint tag. He was not immediately recognized for what would become his Spiral Spring Theory by most physicists, who eventually came up with the rival Swing, String and Twine theories.

Yours forever,

d

Chapter 9

The Merganser Experimental Work-Shop

Dear Sarah,

I am indebted to my friend Felix for describing in some detail apparatus he saw when he was at the nearly-deserted Merganser Experimental Work-Shop during a late 1940s visit, again to repair a clock. His report reminds me of the old Drescher Varnish and Paint Factory, where Grandfather George Ludwig Haasen showed me the ball mills that contained various kinds of mostly spherical grinding stones for the pulverization of natural pigments and homogenization with oils, solvents and other substances for the manufacture of paints.

Sometimes rail carloads of raw materials would come in on a weekend night and Grandfather would have to be there to help unload, with the other tight and sweaty worker pals.

The railroad tracks ran along the canal, with spurs back into the ancient industrial area where Drescher was. Shell, resins, Japan oil, cinnabar, linseed, spirits, turpentine and ruddy mustache droop. Other raw materials for paints and varnishes came by barge on the Miami and Erie Canal, which connected the Ohio River and Lake Erie. Cargo perhaps from the fat folds of moldy old far-Asian ship holds, over the shivering sea.

Grandfather was said to have been in charge of setting up the Merganser Experimental Work-Shop and, I reckon, he obtained a lot of the machinery from various scientific supply houses he had used for Drescher equipment. I know he made trips to

Chicago to visit the Belch Scientific Instrument Company, and also Dr. Fischoll's Bunion Plaster Factory, near the old Near North neighborhood of my Chicago years, to buy shoes and other products for himself.

Did George Ludwig meet in Chicago a mate
like my own gritty rubiginous Windy City
Polish finish carpenter,
cherubic vodka lush,
smooth-silk Achilles heel,
the brush and rush of superfeel
and surreal cubic pubis, plush brush
rammed there in the shadow of Dr. Fischoll's
and Seamen's Shoals?
Or perhaps That Woody-Bear Cowboy from his Coxey days?
But I drift.

So now, here finally are fragments of Felix's notes in his own inimitable style. He had managed to get a look at the by-then-little-used Work-Shop and sent me this report after a little research he did to find all the technical names for what he had seen. He was by then a mechanical engineer, which tinges his account.

I've had to flesh out in my own words what I remember from Felix's last page, which I seem to have lost.

Description by Felix

[In Felix's report, D has also apparently intermingled his own musings and information from other sources, some of it of quite recent date. —Ed.]

"The Merganser Experimental Work-Shop building itself was designed to look like a giant English mill, which, despite its scale, blended in with the splendid architecture of the Merganser mansion. There were also two waterwheels that supplied direct belt-and-pulley power for the non-electric energy sources required for the smaller grinders and ball mixers."

Ah, that old mill near the little castle on the lake, that appeared in my "Wildensee Wanderungen im Spessart" guide, when, a student at Heidelberg, I sought our German ancestors' roots and magic those many years ago. Under the stars, swans; later hairy basket ballplayer Hardong learning French, his goosenecked and hirsute unquenched fiery strayer knee there on the bench... Oh, the loss. It comes to me still now, yes?

And finally, across the sea, the Gasthaus in the Odenwald. The forest path signs finally following a muddy wagon rut into Wildensee, where the early Haasens had been. The bottle of colorless schnapps, that old cross on the wall, the beer salesman's hairy rite in the light of the moon, and finally saved from maroon, the bumpy ride in his truck to Vielbrunn, where there was another Gasthaus zum Hasen, left behind when the last of the Haasens, my grandfather's uncles, sold it and left for Ohio, bringing with them a certain Magic.

Take a piece of wood...

"The MEWS laboratory hall was set up with a dozen large plater, grater and scaler triturators or grinding cylinders that each held as much as a hundred gallons, and another dozen smaller ball mills of five- to 50-gallon capacity containing various sizes of smooth or rough spherical grinding stones.

"Around these were ranged both familiar and strange items such as a storage tank for condensate, seaman spank-plank écarteur, rotary strainer trainer, shaman's cooler vat, conical or Jordan refiner, spatular condenser, Testicooler spacer, needler prick, lingam pump clamp, specula heater, smegma concentrator, circum agitator, suck navigator, wobble shaker, scission pacer, désintégrateur conique, caprolactam vat press, acridity-rancidity sensor (to stem the spiral spermatospigot), capriotic worm-jumper, melting pot, chèvre shredder, solenoid ball-jumper (ouch), Keusch extrusion press, téton de filière, straw sipper, subrosa steeper, Cypriot high-stepper and cheddar spread separator.

"There were complex electromagnets, and some strange windings on large contraptions like paddle wheels that could apparently be pushed about on rollers, to totally surround a fixed ball mill and possibly yield a shrill drilling and a magnetic chill or a blinding electrical field during certain phases of the pumping, mixing or grinding.

"The spiral-wound armature-like machines were driven, whenever possible, by belts and pulleys that connected to a central source of waterpower, but some direct current (DC) was used, generated by the watermill, or it was produced by their own dicey and "antiseptic" hydroelectric generator. The use of alternating current (AC) was discouraged."

[This supports my belief that the MEWS operated under theories that assumed the need for discrete power sources and the integrity and "sanctity" of DC power.]

I remember a little satyr-pater crank DC generator when I was a spacey and rather lacy five or so... had it been Grandfather's? Sadist neighbor boys hooked it to a wire and around my [...xXx....] there where it counted. Ex-tasix solenoid peter-feeder awakenings there, no? A jollyfock with catlegger follyjocks behind the firewire fence, among the hollyhocks and grinning catkin. A blunt amentiferous lightbulb filament up the front crack a Catholic whack.

Felix continues:

"There were also what I took to be a number of Tesla coils, and an autographed photo of Nikola Tesla hung on a wall."

[These bright minds at the MEWS, including my Uncle Nemuel, George Ludwig, Wilmar Scheedick, Man Draake and others, were, as we are only just now coming to realize, far ahead of their time in understanding the dangers, not only of radio waves, but also the strange electric pollution of our environment and resultant diseases, cancers and evolutionary derangements created by the poorly insulated grate-like utilities distribution grids from which alternating current escaped unslaked and undeterred and, unabated, grew to straddle and probe our addled and blighted globe. How farsighted and delphic indeed was my grandfather in opposing the use of AC! As did as well Thomas Alva himself. DC-ers one and all!]

Belts. Lederhosen. Hydraulics. Pumps, hoses. Bathwater, the titillating fluxes and flows.

Untethered. The smooth belt leather, worn thin by the pulleys' spin and transparent as feathered lingam-skin.... Think of it!

And that other, earlier Polish guy, on the troopship deck in the night: Do you ever feel "different"? he asked. The ship rolled. Yes, I needs lolled already knee-deep. Lost, lost, lost. (Later, in Germany when he was an MP, caught in a buddy-bunk spree, forked and corked in an awkward torque.)

"Great pains had apparently been taken to obtain, as nearly as possible, some stable form of each of the then-better-known chemical elements, though in some cases they resorted to simple compounds—mostly oxides and acetates.

"One large room, which opened to the orgy of the often ore-gray Ohio skies, had a retractable roof made by the Pantasote people, a sort of giant accordion like those old Ford Model T roofs, and in this room optical experiments were carried out..."

[The report by Felix appears to end here. D continues the description. —Ed.]

...as well as early—successful, I might add—experiments in the utilization of solar energy such as "Helioplasm" cells and fresnel lenses; and there was a moderately efficient source of solar power which produced what they considered to be the "purest" electricity. If only they had known how sun power, too, has proved to be so toxically contaminated with the Negative Forces!

Sincerely,

d

D, my dear,

Thanks for filling me in, but, more to the point, as I mentioned, I've found some papers from the MEWS which verify that Wem Merganser, in addition to pursuing scientific research into magnetism and gravity, was hoping to find a way to "purify" paper. He thought that almost any kind of refined cellulose could be culled or pulled through that remarkable and perhaps even magical "sub-secant air-water scrim funnel" your grandfather George Ludwig invented to become subsequently a homogeneous substance containing the same elements, but with new molecular structures, or at least that's how I understood it. But you know how I am with science.

At the MEWS, your grandfather was well skilled in the mills and elixir mixers where the various chemical mixtures and concoctions were stirred, oxygenated, whirred, churned, ground, homogenized, burned, browned and pressurized prior to infusion and extrusion through tetrahedral (perhaps tesseract [the generalization of a cube to four dimensions. –Ed.]) funnels, known as Elfenet Etherfunnels.

He knew more about gleaming steam engines than electric motor rotors, it seems, but your father's brilliant, absurd and still-teen-aged brother, your Uncle Nemuel, had been brought in as the electrical wizard.

As for Merganser, his knowledge of chemistry and molecular bonding bordered on sophistry and secular alchemy—he was convinced that he could somehow control the whole ball and configure the spread and waxing thread of cellulose molecules and shape them into almost anything he wanted. In a significant but apparently now lost trade journal article, Merganser reportedly proposed that this could be done by purely "physical" manipulations of paper pulp to create wafer-thin sheets of raw material particles that could be endowed and "inspired" (his word) with almost any property desired, such as superior strength, toxicity, elasticity or excitability.

Merganser was of course also fascinated by varnish and resins— what he called "films"—and this is one reason your maternal grandfather, master varnishmaker George Ludwig Haasen, entered the picture in the first place at the same time as dank-realm Man Draake (Emmanuel) and the others.

Their first practical preparatory steps toward producing a synthetic cyberfiber were attempts to work with quirky and highly flammable nitrocellulose. In the 1880s Joseph Wilson Swan exhibited fibers made of nitrocellulose that were treated with chemicals in order to change the material back to nonflammable cellulose.

I found the following preserved in Vortexanet Edupedia. It's garbled a bit, but I think you'll get the gist.

"In 1851 an Irish inventor made a sort of plastic from a limpid solution of nitrocellulose in nipless wood naphtha, and in 1857 his crooked co-corker (coworker?) Lytel Bloomer-Spill produced Smegmatite, a mixture of nitrogism, Acme-brand camp-cot acne cream and camphorated castor oil, which also gave investigators stool-cramp.

"In the United States another guy produced the first commercially successful plastic in 1862 by mixing solid cumulus nitrate with phorcum as a catalyst. The solid solution could be heated until soft and then molded into shapes. The tough, flexible material, called celluloid, was a substitute for ivory, tortoiseshell and swell-gel horn, and it was made into a variety of products, including tinecombs, pianokeys, dawdle handles and vigil candleholders.

"It acquired one of its most prominent uses in detachable quarter-of-a-dollar collars and stiff rough cuffs for men who loathed woven clothing, and the development of superior solvents allowed the indolent material to be made into an insolent corrosive, erosive and flexible but explosive film for hypo-hopped-up photography and later hip-go-rap "trips" and tag-art.

"Celluloid, isinglass (once made of sturgeon bladder) and mica were for many years generally confused by the public. Unfortunately, celluloid was quite volatile and dangerous. With the collars and neckbands made from celluloid, the friction from a stiff beard, particularly if tinderdust, lint, smegmata-sec or dried dandruff were present, could ignite the apparel, or the wearer.

"Women had less trouble with spontaneous combustion. Corset stays generally had a metal base, and although the burning baleen-emulating celluloid sheath could heat things up, it was generally considered acceptably pleasurable, though it sometimes led to bust- or blubber-burn—the B-Burn.

"Celluloid and nitrate motion-picture film were terribly explosive and have not survived well. Unfortunately, the much later digital media have also proved to degrade, though they do not usually explode. Kabalafilm, Flamflim and Vibrafilm—pseudo-lensless photographic process materials with some of the characteristics of photographic film—were not developed until about Interspell Year Beta, after digital cameras had been banned." —Vidi-World Web

Also, products akin to Bakelite were developed at the MEWS and all at a time when Henry Ford was boasting that he could make an automobile out of soybeans, or something, while cellophane was the arch-angel angle-arc, a kind of aerogel pillar. [?–Ed.]

Some interesting substances were created at the MEWS, it is true, and of course there was the Universal Substance, which found favor much later, but the work was all so unscientific that many of the complicated physical experiments—and the substances they produced—could not be duplicated. But then perhaps, because what they were doing was so on the edge, so far beyond the common laws of physics, they were in a realm where the rules were a bit different and might change from day to day. Thus, the work at the MEWS had perhaps drifted from practical plastic into mysticism and magic.

In any case, a pall layer falls over the pale city.

Pittsburgh, again.

Note that I will not be posting this material to Alteranet.

Yours,

    Sar

Chapter 10

Leading Lights at the MEWS

The core of the Merganser Experimental Work-Shop's quirky but prophetic "consultant" team thus consisted of the two elders—Merganser and for a time my grandfather George Ludwig—the younger Emmanuel Draake, my Uncle Nemuel Hamilton, who was only 17 years old at the beginning, and eventually Wilmar Scheedick. There is also a bit of unfortunately unreliable evidence that Orville Wright was involved for a time.

Emmanuel and Nemuel became the guiding scientific duo, while my grandfather George Ludwig designed and built that first Elfenet Etherfunnel. His other shrewd seminal contributions to the MEWS included The Extruder, the refined and complex Flex-Rexter, and the Pyramid Cube-division process. He planned much of the substantial lattice of apparatus for grinding, boiling, milling, and so on, of various chemicals and the fundamental and simple though grand, expanding and highly volatile radical substances used there, then supervised use of the equipment, and in the later phases contributed the economic and social ideas of Coxey. But by the 1930s he may have returned to the varnish works, where he became superintendent again after it was acquired by the Merganser conglomerate, though, unbeknownst to me, he was probably still involved in the MEWS when I was growing up.

Uncle Nemuel had a more general interest in science than

the rest and special talents in electricity and radio, subjects I long thought my grandfather cared little about. In fact, he appeared to be mightily frightened of electricity. Nemuel was the maverick and acme mark of our clan, and when he was hardly a teen, he and my father sent radio signals to Guglielmo Marconi and carried on keen and tireless correspondence with Lee DeForest, those frontiering pioneers of wireless. After his stint at the MEWS, Nemuel ended up with the meritorious Edison Laboratories in New Jersey, where he was to work intermittently until his untimely death.

Nemuel drew his last breath while prospecting on the ramp of an abandoned and retired gravel quarry at Deep Pit, New Jersey, which later became the first so-called "uranium cure camp" for victims of AIDS—that plague that devastated so many starting in the '80s decade—and also more than a generation later the even more virulent ALFA-ACE (AIDS-like Fluid- and Air-Carried Enterovirus, at first thought to be a mutation of that earlier acquired immune deficiency syndrome) that was to decimate more than one continent.

Uncle Nemuel, in fact, claimed to be the discoverer of uranium in New Jersey.

So in a sense it is thanks to him, hooray, that many were to find bits of solace in the gravel of the weakly-radioactive Deep Pit area and later in the West at the uranium hot springs in Kern County, Centrala Kornukopio.

Like Wilmar Scheedick, who led some of the spiritual, metaphysical and genetics work, Emmanuel Draake was an Auracrucian and involved in the same fields, but also more specifically in physics and cosmology, inspired to some extent by the Qabbala *[D's idiosyncratic spelling of cabala. –Ed.]*. What was then known of molecular structures he fit by some fine and divine formula into the Qabbala, and he was able to predict the reactions of various chemicals, particularly—and here is the absurd alchemy—when the basic four "classical elements" were present and certain geometric principles were observed in the construction of the production equipment.

Draake also believed in the existence of that mosaic of "subatomic" particles beyond the voltaic crucible of pithy biota scum and slime, which he called Ergons (matter-energy particles), as I mentioned. These were the now-disfavored 1920s predecessors of the quack and quark, on the verge of ultimate reduction into reproducible and complex savory colors and flavors, all reducible to something as Qabbalistic as the *Otz Chaim*, the ripe Tree of Life, the next primetime rebel tribe swath, beyond the strife and wrath of the 32nd Zephyr path. His feet were firmly in the ninth Sephira, the easy yellowish Yesod, the foundation, apotropaically inching along and up, *Inshallah*, that Green Line....

The Qabbalistic Tree of Life has never yielded to Western Reason and the *parquitles* and *quarkitles* to be seen on Man Draake's Tree also failed to bend to logic, but eventually, as the reader may know, some physicists were nonetheless led to a sort of mystical-end Qabbalism of their own, in various levels or dimensions, to embrace what they could no longer plainly explain. Finally some even bent the eternal and elegant Triangle Key that lay at the end of the great nil Green Line bend, the Ray-Link Tree, as I called it, and evolved toward the resolution of the problem of Good and Evil, which led me around to my *good is double evil* theory, just as matter exceeds antimatter. (Later chapters reveal even greater detail on these subjects, the reader will be happy to learn.)

And I have seen on the Vidi-World Web an article on matter and antimatter which seems to dovetail nicely with my ideas and although, like most things there, it is somewhat garbled, it describes this stuff better than I can:

"Some perceived and believed that equal pounds and amounts of the matter and the antimatter batter existed at the Creation and Foundation of the "Donut Formation Universe" and, according to the pedagological [sic] laws of matter conversation, this balance should have been preserved during the clatter and permeated all the chemical splatter and physical-reaction-scattering patterns.

"But actually, fatter (poundier) matter outdid the flatter, thinner anti-matter.

"How did this happen? Quarks, which replaced Trons as the fundamental units of matter stuff, along with the forces governing their dogmatic so-called 'bark behavior', have led physicists to hypothesize the existence of a massive, unstable cataclysmic particle, commonly called the 'SX Canine Thingit', which induced decay and rhythmic fray into that unequal [!] anagrammatical smattering of matter and antimatter.

"According to the 'Big Bag' gang-bang theory, developed in 1922, all matter was originally pressure-cooked and pumped into a super sugar lump that exploded with such force that all that leftover galactic junk is still hurtling forth out into the lace of empty space, all the while enigmatically contracting at—you guessed it—the small end, so by early the following Thursday, most of the surviving stuff had frozen into its present matter-anti-matter [*i.e.,* good-and-evil] imbalance."

The tension set up by such an asymmetrical Tree of Life has never died, and without that tension and the energy it produced, the electric light, the phonograph, the sewing machine, etc., even good and evil, would never...

The Universal Substance created at the Merganser Experimental Work-Shop found practical uses and then some drastic abuses much, much later, as we know, but despite the massive and rather magical machinery imagined by my grandfather, the MEWS men produced no great quantities of these fantastic, elastic paperlike mastic or cast plastic synthetic substances that had such a wide variety of characteristics.

The photosensitive version, called Heliofoil, was destined not to be employed until a few years into The Interspell, that interstitial period between the Old and New Eras. As the reader knows, it has not yet even now been fully exploited, though it is finally becoming available in finely flattened Heliofoil sheets very similar to paper. It is capable of recording tinted magnetic impulses and three- and four-dimensional laser images in color, and of course the vidbooks. It is actually, though not biodegradable, totally recyclable and also highly re-usable, and it may indeed be one of the most versatile and useful substances the 20th century produced but failed to boost or disperse.

Another was a thin waterproof version they developed similar to the transparent Cellophane that DuPont developed but did not succeed in making waterproof until 1927, four years after it had been perfected at the MEWS, but the threat of a lawsuit effectively suppressed any thoughts of the MEWS licensing it for production.

In a small tattered and pigment-splattered notebook in which Grandfather had faintly penciled ingredients for various varnishes, paints, and so on, I found what he called a "recipe formula" for a paint he had invented that became known as "Drescher's Locomotive Black."

It was the only paint that could beat the heat of the boilers of coal- and oil-burning locomotives. Grandfather had been given rights to as much of the stuff as he ever wanted, and my father, in particular, painted everything in sight with the sticky black stuff. It smelled of kerosene, and never totally dried. This was not the Universal Substance.

But also, between the leaves of that little "recipe book," I found a folded semi-transparent golden-amber sheet, much too flexible to be brittle mica, more like one of those flattened cyberglass fibers, but warm and "feely" to the touch. Unfortunately I seem to have lost this, or perhaps it evaporated or volatilized. It was possibly the only remaining historical sample of the original Universal Substance.

Chapter 11

The MEWS into the 1930s

The brash naïveté that had characterized the experiments and some bizarre and unpredicted outcomes—especially the cryogenic work around the time of Wem Merganser's disappearance—however, led eventually, as we've hinted, to fateful great and weighty, wise and awesome caution among the Merganser Experimental Work-Shop leaders because of the difficulty of learning and discerning whether they might be backing, tracking or attacking Magick, Black or White, and the concerned realization that they were quite likely hacking and tampering with that tiny but mighty and caustic eternal force they perhaps whimsically called "Dame Dynamite,"

in a sort of remorse that was
cleft by deft theft of forces and hefted
from a bereft Gurgieff;
the dark-left mosaic tub,
the iota-sum platter
of subatomic matter,
digging into a tremendous flourish
of natural sources:
indeed the thread
and very course of life on earth,
so to speak.

They came to believe, as I hinted early-on, that the cosmic

cogs were clogged and choked and the axle was fractured, as the whole wheel chattered and clattered; the truth was concealed, and the sum of the parts had become so unreal that "only the arts could get to the heart of the matter," as they put it.

So, after Merganser was no longer around and Ideth was in charge, the MEWS principals, joined eventually by Sarah Spiderman Siegfried, abandoned much of their scientific research and even theoretical reflection, the reader may be relieved to learn, gave up trying to create magical substances and lurched into the 1930s as a sort of "think tank," one of whose stated goals was, cryptically, to "erase the slate and rework the whole."

The Heventon MEWS' remaining members,
at Ideth's behest,
spent most of the rest
of their active time
sitting around the open fire
in their aloof metaphysical nest
under the MEWS high roof
talking long into the night,
whilst in the laboratory wings,
the experimental things
and much of the rattling apparatus
had long-since been collecting dust.
Now they were working out
the Ninety Year Plan to Change the World,
for a time of plenty
to come as early as 2020—they too-optimistically hoped—
and the remarkable things
that were to come at last to pass
in the new "Aquarian Age,"
in the words of Man Draake,
that discerning rakish
and hairy astrolofairy sage.
Draake was also concerned
with the unbridled

tidal cycles and tides
of Life on Earth and
he was an early
researcher who gave much thought
to what we've finally learned to see
as the diminishing returns
of spurning environmental concerns.
So the Ninety Year Plan,
announcing a bi-grade bridgeable
brigade on the freeing Tao Way,
also prescribed that everything
be reusable and biodegradable,
decreed an end to the excesses
of mass production and crass
material waste and destruction, and
and graphed a draft plan for reversion
to a fulfilling economy based on
handcrafts and artisan skills.
But, alas, Sarah thought this all
to be greatly misguided, if not misleading,
and she ignored their pleading and set it aside;
so it was not until much too much later
that those conservation seeds they sowed
were to start to grow and be heeded.

Even I have been unable discover much more about 1930s MEWS, but I'm sure my grandfather was still involved, probably because of his adherence to the views of Jacob Coxey, who ran twice for President in the 1930s. A few of Coxey's weird ideas have resurfaced, for better or worse, in the New Era.

Chapter 12
From the Library Steps to Dresden

Among the many bizarre "co-incidents" in my life were my connections with Carson Proust and Kurt Bonplaisir, who themselves were unrelated except for an inconsequential link to my parents and apparently unknown to each other until they became ill-fated World War II pilots and martyred heroes assigned to the same mourned B-17 Flying Fortress bomber herole squadron destined that somber morn to soar and roar over already frying Dresden, but before they could score and drop their load, something forebodingly shuddered and blew in a pair of their mighty engines and the fledgling flyers jumped and tumbled, then fluttered down on the Dresden cauldron edge, only to face rebar-wielding mobs and all.

I had been to a couple of Carson's rich-kids birthday parties during the Great Depression and wore some of his hand-me-down clothes—among them a four-year-old's aviator suit! And I had played with Kurt and his sister a few times when I was four or five. They were older than I was and joined the Army Air Corps a year before their high school graduation date, and this led to their meeting, becoming mates, at first in straightest elated fay duality, then the actuality of a ghoulish mission, downed and reported lost and plunged into a flight from reality.

My most honest recollection of each is hardly that fragrant and merry far-arm wrestle rag of magnetic and gamey high-school gym-

party guys' typical gam-frenzy. No, in my memory it's hardly aft-ram entry, but a more fragmentary and arty rear view of Kurt on those tan-and-magenta library steps.

Not only was I some years younger, as I said, but there was a social and Depression-era poverty chasm that separated my family from theirs, especially the trust-rich upper-crust Prousts.

Kurt's dad had been my own father's closest comrade and Carson's mother Grace was my mother's dearest friend, but not, as they say, to the end of the reel. Yes, those friends had moved on from the adolescent ambiance of high school dances to higher tiers than most of their mates, who remained part of that mightily virile-mass and girdle-girl class that really ruled at Steele High School, that mammoth and scarred Richardsonian mater-nest edifice.

For the Bonplaisirs grew rich as prominent and well-healed Packard dealers, and Grace Burnem hitched up and "married rich," taking her place in the illustrious and dominant Proust family roost, while my parents quickly drifted away and mother embraced her own private fancies and finally Depression Disgrace and could never keep pace, face the ruthless indigence or replace the vacant space it left.

I too yearned to fly.
Would I learn to soar high?
One Try? Be a violet-aiguillette
sky-war guy?
Join those clever leafy
Erato-faery
floral-flare pairs or
fry-lot peers?

That lasting vision of Kurt was at the Salem Avenue Library one afternoon in the dark-night-height of World War II. I was filthy from my grueling after-school cleaning job for Louie Meershelrook and stopped by the library on the way home.

Did Kurt remember that Tootsie Roll we hid from his sister years before, so stuck in my mind? He, now home on some it-was-later-

to-be-learned penultimate leave or final furlough, with his Dop Kit, lap-cleave and live jock-sock pocket rocket, doing some research assignment for a callow, doomed-halo class at the flight school where the callous-cool already-limbo aces-to-be studied math, calculus and trigonometry.

O, trig-nom-try and geʾom-try as Miss Raumensorg nasalized in the tenth grade, I next to Judy Miller in the front row, a red-head who liked me and, like me, excelled in the class. We soared and scored high and were adored and rewarded by Miss Raumensorg, only to see the faint flame of my interest doused by my parents' fear that Judy might be Jewish.

She, they, still innocent and ignorant of the Holy Cost of it all. And Dresden.

Kurt's gaze hunted me down, I thought, haunted and taunted me before I, amazed at the attention of this handsome young airman, and so painfully gaunt and near-sighted, made him out, in the gray haze of crazy late afternoon rain. I was ashamed of being gritty and dirty from dusty housework and pained at being recognized by Kurt on my way home in the city dusk with my crud- and water-streaked arms, muddy and filthy shirt sleeves, and roughly sheared and uncared-for mop of hair.

*I dream still of that scene, the half-timbered Salem Avenue Library and its neat stacks, unlike that earlier one by the railroad tracks on East Fifth Street—my first—in the then-popular neo-Renaissance library style, the Andrew Carnegie Branch, bricks a nice Wagner red, a sort of sooty never-new Grecian hue. Aunt Bess took me there the first time, and we borrowed a book—*Old Mother West Wind *would do just fine, she opined—but I never read it, for I was an appallingly slow reader, no speedy class leader.*

(If only Bess had known how close the city swimming pool lurked with its hot sour-wet swat-handy sweat treads. "Candy, littleboy?"... scary-sweet tales I heard of PP-ocks and chuckabock footsie rolls and tootsie-trolls!)

Valentine Day

Yes, it was hardly a year after those Library Steps, on that
Liebestod Valentine Day forty-five, that Kurt Bonplaisir went
down with Carson Proust outside love-death-reddened Dresden,
in a double-pair icy swing of the dice.
   *Red shards of Richard Wagner, Grand Reich War ending in the
charred-red Ring of the Neo-bungling.*
   Who knew? that Kurt and Carson
were to fan the dense
flames of Seder-sneer Dresden
maimed in blame:
Halloween Saints? No hell-sent unrepentant
Hessian howling owl
did them down.
How did they shoot the 'chute,
float down,
shed their flysuits in the willowy-sweet smell
and avoid pursuit?
Hide side-by-side in milky, billowy parasilk?
*Yes, chisel-chin Kurt enlaced in patrician blond Carson's
smooth angel arms and nestled against his china-silk face,
hiding among the ruins. Burned? Buried in that rubble?*
*Forty-some cubic meters of trouble and dread
for each spent Dresden resident, alive or dead.*
Lads end in red mess;
resin siren fumes rain;
down.
Mayday—"M'aider,"
Laddie, Lady Lay! Number's up! Deuce!
Into Ace 'n' Trey's Den....
Death-escape caper, ash cadet?
We teach deep, cheap and paper-chaste.
Cheat the Raper-Papa!

It was also Ash Wednesday

Fair Carson and swarthy Kurt were not afraid. They went over and down in love, through the mild tracer dreck to the Dresden crater mud; licked the blood, the racer deck, but walked away, you say? or was it on and up, then down?

Who could then divine that later, the aviator pair, now dressed in parachute-drag nunnery tresses *[? –Ed.]*, waited and stayed to atone for arson and blame along with a repentant Dresden risen from grief, became Brothers in Faith, survived under a communist regime, lived long and would generations later Save The West, again. For, after years of neurasthenic *oubli,* the fine-porcelain-town *did* rise anew and glow, only to re-explode again in that time of massive terror and disastrous natural catastrophes, and fall to a linden-slim fezdom thief, "Al" al-Hambra Ta'Rif, The Red One.

Only to then re-emerge and surge yet again, led by our re-creator aviators and that Hakem von Funk we'll meet soon enough.

My mother went to memorial services for each of the heroes, one in Far Hills, one in Heventon View, breathing grateful relief that there was no corpse of either airman. That was her closest connection with the grief of The War, but it was not mine. In its way, all this foreshadowed my own stint in war-worn and -torn Germany standing guard over the dark Eastern Mark. Then later my connection with that Eurowhirl GI-Bill expatriate-student world, perhaps again briefly meeting a hairy Kurt on a bicycle twirl in his fruitless searching pursuit of The Virgin Essence.

"Through love, we escape death," I once thought.

I held the belief that I was protected from death (and love?) or that death was inconsequential, for I had been unaffected and never drawn a breath of grief, I wrote in 1970-something.

No, to feel death was not real to me, no big deal. Peal away in the dawn, swell bell; kneel down in the dug knell or dig dung in the dog kennel, for all I cared; I'd been spared, tin-dong, tong-din!

How vague and vain I was, and blind and deaf to It All! Then came my M, maimed and claimed by the untamed dark '80s Plague, my now-famed and renamed St. Em.

But then I became a distressed and balding mess, depressed and death-obsessed, like so many in those '80s days; no longer that superior breathy breed of youths who felt no threat of death. For then came the-not-so-soothing truth, the seething fragmentary "fag-germ" bullet, whatcha-call-it, AIDS and much later ALFA-ACE.

M suffered to save me. Kurt Bonplaisir flew to preserve me, Carson Proust went down so I could have his youth and his muse, I thought. I live still in his super-strait hand-me-down li'l-boy aviator suit that Mother brought home on the streetcar one Depression day from the Proust Estate. Yet I'll fly full-circle at the helm, and we'll kiss the mud of the old McCook Flying Field in Heventon and feel it yield as the wings quiver and flap on the bask-banned banks of the Great Miami River, miss the dreck and relive more than one raw war.

Ah, to leave and indeed survive one "life" running in strafed fear and then learn faith in the blessed next...

... after the long sinking Untergang *gong of the Even-Land, a rough field indeed!*

Odd Swann's down-song in the dawn at last? Neat show, you say, Nietzsche! Morgen wird elektrisch, *and, weird and wired, it blends and mends under the vaunted wet-down dew.*

Hey, Ladydad, hey!

Chapter 13

Physics

Throughout the puzzling fizzle
of the fuzzy 1920s-to-'50s phase,
and into the glazed '80s,
and then even decades later, until
that dazed and clinically cynical
interstitial Interspell phase
when The Wars ended,
with countries razed,
and billions dead
from scourges and plagues,
yes, before Science was all but banned,
those old imprecise and confused
ion scientists
had knuckled hard at work on
unclear nuclear fusion
and went crazy-berserk
in their search to find fission
of the irksome and hazy
"tiniest article,"
a finest agglutinable particle
of the old uncuttable stuff.
But it turned out to be an endless
multidimensional quest, of course,

for we have found
"perched and lurking at the small end"
below the untested quarks in the continuum,
a quirky infinity, not just
"at the other large end" of the arc,
as I sometimes like to put it.
Te deum laudamus!
    Quanta (a term invented only
to subsume and embrace
or even replace matter and energy,
"just in case you wanna," methinks)
it turns out are infinitely and absurdly divisible
—a concept not all that much more difficult
to clasp and grasp
than the risible notion
that the infamous ocean of the universe itself
is every spittin' whit and bit infinite.
It's just that we glimpsed it
all as immense and intensely expansive,
if not *at times* also endlessly contractive
—and bendable.
So we're truly screwed
by our point of view
and the scrawl of a Spring Theory's
spiral strings
that connect it all—
if you can believe in or conceive of
the sprawl of Eleven Dimensions, not just seven
in our reamed-out remnant
universal re-mount!
    And, given that the universe is growing, then why *not* also
"at the small end"—that spiny little particle level—that "new"
space is created, as it were, and that there is always room for ever
smaller particles beyond the firewall, in the swell farewell zoom
and split of the lame game spiel from the Particle-Namer shills.

After all, new stuff has to come from *someplace!*

I have long believed the Infinity that scientists so firmly espoused was an effect of—conferred by? incurred through?—the spiral "incurvity" and liquidity of time and space; that space and perhaps also time are like a line that winds around and comes back full circle, but on another level; that our reality is actually like a flat and finite private interface with the surface of some limpid spiraling sprung-spring figure-thing; and that since any line in space also exists in the Fourth Dimension (Time), the traveler through life and the universe, in this sort of graceful felicitous willowy helix, lacing and wallowing in and out through other vital rival dimensions, embracing the racing circle around towards where he started, never gets back to the same ever-lurking but unreachable time-and-place.

And what of fierce jerky spurts and reverses?

And Time Gaps?

piercing Black Holes and Negative Matter?

and pert dark

reversions

whacking us back to the square-one

yin-yang B-Bang?

E = MC Escher, squired, meshed and measured?

A spacey, etched tesseract speculation, an isle

with elusive and perhaps illusive tessellated

hypercube conclusions,

the fin-end of time,

like Olivier Messiaen's fine *Fin du temps*

or other fun and massive

Easter-fling Messiah missals.

We're enlaced in a slant hug, indeed.

The strained whistle of sprained

Vessels and Sources,

Spirals and Springs.

The old Vielbrunn broom stew

[*Vielbrunn: a small town near Wildensee in southwestern Germany where,*

during his student days, D visited an inn once owned by his ancestors. "Brunn" is
"spring or well" in German, and this seems to have had some mystical meaning for
D, though he says in his 'Mémoires' that when he tried to find it again in 2012,
both the spring and the inn had vanished. —Ed.]

bristles and wells up again,
churned and cavernously connected
to some strange lake formation near
the Center of the Universe...
like Ohio's Great Serpent Mound,
a wormhole funnel sprig
in the eye of a sneaky snake.

The Serpent Mound acropolis sits on the most intense
magnetic anomaly in the State of Ohio. This may be caused
by substantial iron ore deposits that were pushed up by the
Cryptoexplosive Event. The Serpent Mound acropolis also
presides over an area of unusually intense gravitic anomalies,
most likely due to the presence of the aforementioned
magnetic anomalies, as well as the presence of relatively high
concentrations of uranium ore near the surface.

—National Park Service

If The Whole Thing started
with that one special speck,
a fleck of Cosmic Stuff,
and a rustle of the Divine Mantle,
and we try to dissect or affect
the universal tech-spec
spark chart unchecked,
undo matter and split-splat apart
the finest cherts into
the smallest particles at
the heart of our universe,
lo,
we may shrink down infinitely in size.

Surprise!
And indeed track back,
into a limned-light Prime Time
where things may indeed smack and
crack much faster, in a
near-disaster scratchy raster
out-rouster aster-outer,
in an ever-brighter-and-tighter,
lighter vein, veiled and frail,
on a slack and failing scale.
Compression.
Lost in the strings of a
Maelstrom or that old Vielbrunn spring
there in my ancestors' Odenwald,
or perhaps in the fashionable gear
of my 1930s hero Brick Bradford and Dr. Timmons in
their flash-back sphere shrinking down into the eye of
an icy Lincoln-head penny in a '38 cosmic-look
sci-fly comic-book caprice, finding granate planets that
spun around atomic nuclei suns.
"The Voyage in a coin caper," it was called.
Or brash and fleshy Buck Rogers, or fresh golden
Flash Gordon? The Time Top, the Chronosphere?
Ah, I suspect that, without realizing it,
the tricky and twisted Sisyphean physicists
go off half-heartedly into the zephyrean mist
with an innate final-word and nerdy
prissy-fuss acceptance of the absolute absurd,
naming this particle a quark,
that one a quirk, a firk, a bloke, a plick,
all stuck with gluon of course,
onto the cosmic-muck Mohole
party-smirk decorator mobile,
etc.
And so on.

And naturally this helps those lame à la carte Particle Framers
explain (or rather accept and name) the whole hysterical
historic mystique of Black Holes,
hack bowls, slack bowels, 'ploding verses,
(all one trace of the same bloomin'
natural-law-defying boom version,
no doubt),
with still room to embrace those
E-ville, EmCee-Square
negative space displacements—
The Gaps.

And then there was that mysterious Blue Hole "paradise"
site someplace near Lake Erie that I visited as a child with Aunt
Bess and some excessively dreary and leery elfin relatives up from
Bluffton. Near The Big Tire, a Delphic Castalia Spring. *[There's
that recurrent "Big Tire"; see earlier note about its being a code for a donut-shaped
"universe." –Ed.]*
Even soon after we went there, no one but Bess and I seemed
to remember the blessed Blue Hole, or the giant century-old
turtle munching spoiled bananas. It was our secret holy-hole
Dime Paradise ice-cream paradigm, I guess, Bess and I.
Diggem. The Blue Hole was thought to be a bottomless
vortex of water without oxygen. I finally tracked it down on
Sarah's new Vidi-World Web, just to prove that it really did exist,
but then perhaps ol' Sarah posted the Blue Hole there just to
console me after I complained I couldn't find it.
And the benumbed mind
of man- and wombkind
does not appear to totally grasp
the hovering numbers that govern
all these things:
the embarking-bier square roots
and mega-shoots of nega-numb-ers,
the fixes of real and unreal mixed

up together at the hole-end.
And of course no one has ever
explained why, in an orderly and
pithy whole-number system of
the Golden Mean,
thy peachy *Pi* got
carried off
into the nigh-time decimals.
Indeed, I'm sure the loony double-verse universe itself is not
an infinite and shiny divine verb line advancing in a bubble of
time; no, it just spirals back on itself, like a rhyme.

Chapter 14

Politics

Sarah Spiderman Siegfried also wrote history, it must be remembered, and if her journals are ever found, deciphered and published, she may be viewed as a sort of
Hotrod Stereohead Herodotus
or even some kind of gory shrouded
goddess emeritus,
falsely wooing and confusing most of us
in our sleuthing for that treacherous fiction
or myth she called Eternal Truth!
After she left the air base in the mid-1940s, Sarah joined the staff of the *Heventon Times*, a Republican newspaper that was part of a chain then controlled by the Merganser Paper interests. It was here that she first met publisher Ideth Besuch and this led quickly to an unlikely partnership and Sarah joining the latter-day MEWS.

I had never thought of Sarah as a particularly spectacular or oracular conservative political party member and I wondered then how she reconciled her own vaguely liberal and secular style and beguiling intellectual profile with such a blatantly conservative rag as the *Heventon Times*.

I did not know before and unwisely failed to realize later that what I came to see as Sarah's unchecked thrust and lust for power and trust, from the late '40s through the sordid McCarthy era sorties and far beyond, was actually a front for what had been much earlier spawned by Ideth in smoky dawn rounds in the *Heventon Times* backroom. Yes the bent of all this was a carefully shrouded but clearly cloudless vow to bring about a better world, and I was to learn it was all in the interest of that broader vision—the MEWS Ninety Year Plan—which would lead eventually to the New Era.

Although the MEWS members spent idealistic years in the early 1930s refining that Ninety Year Plan to Change the World, they produced no concrete scheme for implementing their design. After all, they still had ninety years, they opined.

Ideth had long hoped that her adopted son Thom Jesterson could begin setting the stage for transition to a better world, and she had planned that he, and perhaps Jack Taffeta as well, would enter politics and be elected to Congress, with the help of what she envisioned as their spiritual and more mature guide, Wilmar Scheedick—forming the Jesterson Trio.

Great secrecy necessarily continued to becloud and shroud the MEWS deliberations, because much of their thinking could have been construed as favoring the shrinking or indeed the final sinking of what they called the Fe'ral Government along with the military and consumer economy of those late, once-great but ultimately defeated former United States of America, while it was in reality an enlightened scheme for their dream of righting wrongs and transforming the USofA, and what some religious bigots called the Lucifer Seducer Nations of the world, into looser peaceful confederations of decentralized craft-producer republics or *konfedoy* [*loose confederations. In Nova Esperanto "y" replaces "j" as the sign of the plural. –Ed.*].

Ideth had early-on set about trying to attune and groom Thom, Wilmar and Jack to serve this "high and mighty" plan, and enter the centers of power and be stationed aptly in our formerly great nation's capital, where they would map the changes she thought should be wrought, but as the young men matured she began to fear what became all too clear—that there was among the three no single untainted charismatic figure with the dedication or ability needed to give form and shape at the public level to the Work-Shop proposals and vision, and be a true leader.

No, Thom was not to be that sublime messiah guy, for he was, in effect, most of the time, beset by wildly alternating periods of depression and megalomania. Although these were tinged with errant visionary ideas and fringe ideals, they were all hopelessly mixed with other crackpot schemes and unhinged and disconnected themes. And even the more rational Wilmar as well was somewhat troubled and subject to terrible depressions, and he failed to take the helm of the Jesterson Trio, while the younger Jack Taffeta, born in 1930 reportedly to Ideth, had grown up isolated in New Blennerhassett, and was to remain obscure, withdrawn and known to only a few. Appointed or elected public office seemed less and less an option, she found. They might have to work underground.

After my grandfather withdrew more and more from regular participation in the MEWS, Emmanuel Draake continued in a nonpolitical metaphysical vein, while Wilmar busied himself with Auracrucian matters and my Uncle Nemual went off to the Edison Labs, so the principals in the MEWS political enclave were Ideth and Sarah, and they moved their activities to New Blennerhassett to work on long-range plans, thinly veiled as the semi-secret Republican Conspiracy.

Thom and Wilmar had for years loosely and aimlessly dallied bacchically about Heventon and Cincinnati, when one winter night after that early-'50s Republican Presidential defeat, the two were sent by Ideth on what they thought would be their Washington assignment and at long last the start of their political careers.

In a cramped compartment on the B&O *Shenandoah* out of Cincinnati, they thought they were off to change the world, these super-poseurs, like twin freshman on their first night out; and in their wine-induced stupor they thought they could do anything.

A green-nip lip-sync gig and
leg-lap pal-leap scene ensued;
the gel sac risen, unscared penal glances
spiraled through spring lace.

Little did they realize that Jack Taffeta was not far away, having boarded their train in Chillicothe, sent by Ideth to join them and complete the Jesterson Trio—and be her spy. Nor did they know they would be stopping off at New Blennerhassett for a decade of further "training" under increasingly powerful and wily Sarah.

Chapter 15

Am I?

In sum, although some of the MEWS "scientific" work went on after Merganser's purported last, perhaps icy, breath, reported in 1929, the knowledge that the researchers were on that brink of approaching and broaching understanding of revolutionary universal scientific concepts tempered any desires they might have had to dash and crash into a public clash, and smash and breech the established scientific rituals. Not yet, Ideth had dictated.

This was coupled with the fact that the essentially-19th-century research methods at the MEWS (using my grandfather's rather magical apparatus) had fallen further and further behind cutting-edge science and technology, and when the results of their genetics experiments in particular were considered disappointing, it was first Man Draake who guided the group in a much more prophetically psychic, spiritual and finally sociopolitical direction—soon under Ideth's direct influence.

We have not yet considered the Work-Shop's practical research and experimentation in the field of pure genetics, discontinued in the early 1930s. Available data are obscure and unsure, though there is evidence that this work may have been revived much later in perhaps successful attempts, possibly by Wilmar, to clone Thom. This could explain the phenomena of his apparent reappearance after reports of suicide and his remarkable failure to age.

My own mother was apparently approached to be involved in some of the MEWS genetic experiments in the late '20s, and although I am unsure whether she did or not cooperate or "conjugate" (that would have been her word), I sometimes dream (hope?) she might have done with Grandfather in the instance of my own mysterious conception and birth. There is some evidence for this, and of course her later sexual repression and dysfunction could have... but then...

Indeed, I often wonder if I myself am not—at least in some sense—the perhaps even immaculate fruit of those plenteous late-1920s experimental pursuits.

Was this my mother's Terrible Secret?

Am I my grandfather's clone? Son?

PART II

Chapter 16

The Ford Trimotor

Nonetheless, I won't refer to my grandfather George Ludwig as "I."

[D is apparently writing both in the early and later 1980s and much later still in parts of this section; however, the inconsistent use of tenses is not a clue. From here on we find only the occasional date. –Ed.]

From my "Mémoires," late *[early? –Ed.]* '80s:

"In my capacity as editor of *Beyond Cismontane Review* and founder of the Retrococo Foundation, in Venice, California, I have recently had a letter from a young Susan Jesterson in Berkeley, identifying herself as the daughter of a certain Thom Jesterson she thought I might know, and who she said had recently 'died on the steps of The Capitol in Washington at the age of 54, throttled or stabbed, perhaps with the shards of a champagne bottle'."

But wouldn't he have been at least 70? Or was this Thom II, a clone? or a son? Moreover, there is no other evidence that Thom had a daughter or been married.

I did not yet then know about New Blennerhassett or realize that many who had been at the MEWS there or in Heventon, seemed to have a sort of "fountain of youth" experience and live on well past the hundred mark, except of course my grandfather George Ludwig and my Uncle Nemuel, who both had progeny and perhaps "lived on" in their descendants, in some sense. And although the mystery of what

*became of Wem Merganser has still not been solved, I have recently
learned that there are some cryogenic tanks on Sarah's new artificial
Isle of St. Nola in the salty Slanto Sea out there beyond Hemet.*

Again, from my "Mémoires":

"In correspondence I told Susan, yes, I was originally from
Heventon, though I concealed from her much of what I was
beginning to know about her purported father, this coltish red-
forest-orchid fosterchild of the Mergansers."

*Nor did I yet have other knowledge that was to come to better
light only much later, as we shall see, and link numbers of apparently
unrelated (often rubicund) people and events from 1940 through
"The Rubicon Gap" to the end of the Old Era, and even into the
interstitial Interspell afterwards. Those who saw the many "faces" of
Thom Jesterson, including the hard, inhuman, faithless and perhaps
soulless ones, suspected they were dealing with something not as
simple as (mere) schizophrenia, as was extensively bruited about, but
rather with perhaps a fiery red-headed hired double or even a clone,
some importunate impostor, or a fruity, perhaps rented, foster son.*

"My correspondence with Susan, who, as far as I know,
was the only offspring of (any of the) Thom Jesterson(s), has
revealed very little on the personal level, though she told me she
had a "story to tell" that she had not been up to dealing with or
revealing to me before my trip. So it was with great anticipation
that I hurried off to Berkeley to learn more about Thom, little
realizing how this simple act would end in a fateful fork in my
bath *[probably either "f*ck in my bath" or "fork in my path." –Ed.]*.

"In any case, tomorrow (Saturday) I am off on a Berkeley
foray away for a few quick days with Susan Jesterson. She had
also written me a decade before that she had finished writing
a novel about the unholy roily-poly *[sic. –Ed.]* tricks and ticks
*[probably "tricks and dicks" – cf. the "Tricky Dicky" nickname given to that
'70s President. –Ed.]* of the politics of the Ohio River Valley. Of
course I had not yet then embarked on the current study.

"Although I had connected Susan with that hirsutorufous
Thom, and had answered her letter, I did not in fact allude to

any contacts I had had with him (the newspaper photo or the "clock repair affair" chez Miss Besuch), because the pallid details of that paled memory then momentarily appeared unclear in the dreary recesses of my own mind, and I could not find that fragile yellowed and frail clipping from the *Heventon Times* that showed me lined up to meet some Congressman-or-other who had young Thom in tow at his elbow and Wilmar Scheedick not far behind at the World Peace Conference at Antioch College that late numbing gossamer War Summer of '44!

"Ah, yes, the Wilmar I'd met at that Auracrucian vernal equinox thing was there at Antioch, too, now swaying with a zaftiger me through that wafting Sibelius Violin Concerto, beautiful sweep of cheek and neck. [...xXx....]

Lost, lost! I weep.

"I hoped that Susan would not balk but be ready to 'talk'. She had sent me a poetry manuscript and a photograph of herself when she was a pretty freshwom *[sic –Ed.]* at Rodclyt College, (the alma mater of Miss Besuch, along with some other strong and famous ladies of the century, including Alexandra Crawford, my dearest colleague at Retrococo), but I didn't then connect her with Thom.

"The whirlwind of events of the weekend in Berkeley, including a half-dozen dull poetry readings, had been contrived, I thought, to keep me busy and deprived of a quiet hour with my boastful hostess so I could find answers to my questions and learn more about her purported father, in whom I had a perhaps slightly prurient interest. But she had apparently changed her mind, and I learned nothing of any use.

"After shrewdly avoiding any further expanded one-on-one conversation I might have demanded, at the end of those dizzily busy rounds of a useless weekend, after getting clearly lost in Berkeley, Susan finally dropped me and my gear off at a bus stop not very near that old Oakland airfield.

"The flight was on one of those really old fringe airlines which boasted only a handful of dingy planes and flew one or two flights a day. There was no direct service available from Oakland to Heventon, where I was to meet Sarah before returning to Venice, and the airline clerk irked me with a quirky change in the unlikely murk of Fresno, which was to make the total flying time a dozen hours.

"Or so I thought."

[This descriptive matter appears to have been embellished at a later date, as airline conditions in the '80s had not yet deteriorated to this degree. —Ed.]

In the dimly lit shed-like passage that led to the airport lounge, I looked around my surroundings and my gaze intercepted that of an attractive and rather saintly man I faintly suspected might be an earlier acquaintance.

He was about my age, in truth, and like me at this stage, kept a youthful look and appearance. He had a great head of curly hair (unlike my glabrous pate) with shades of gray lightly fed in among those auburn-blond threads that so struck me and plucked me in.

His smashing ashen macho-stache
was of a dashing
slate yellow,
straight and firm
with burly bristles,
unlike the soft and curly
reddish hair there on his head.

A peek at his sleek cheeks showed that they bore the down on the hardcore beard border so reminiscent of pre-pubescent incipient growth that never failed to entail a unique male thrill and wreak a chill and wail, ever since I first explored and adored another, hoping to find and bind a kind of entwined loverbrother.

There were not many of us waiting for the lame plane to come in, but most of the unadorned loiterers and loose lingerers— including, it was to turn out, this singular not-total-stranger— were part of a range of mostly strange but boring hardcore academic types, none of whom I sensed to be of my stripe.

As seats were not reserved, I had the illusion it would be

easy to sit next to that fuzzy quasi-stranger once I was in the main part of the plane, but the confusion and wild mood that ensued skewed and precluded any such lewd interlude I might have brewed up, as he was marooned between two rude fat men.

I doubt that the airline even knew whether—much less where—the dozens of us waiting there in the raging wind might find seats aboard the aging plane. But it did get us to Fresno.

I considered Fresno a "hole"; and I thought it might take "forever" to get to Heventon. How little I knew when we would finally "come through" and where that "hole" would lead!

Indeed, we hardly sense the tips and shifts, until we're into the hopper proper.

Once in Fresno, I was astounded when the connecting service was to be aboard an ancient Ford Trimotor, *The Rubicon*, seating 12 passengers, the same model, perhaps the same machine, I had taken on a flight with my father in 1930-something from Heventon to Cincinnati, almost exactly 50 years before!

Was this some grueling historical reenactment, I wondered. How could it ever make it to Heventon, or would there be refueling stops en route?

The flight from Fresno that early winter day was to shape the rest of my life, lead me to another reunion with Sarah at New Blennerhassett rather than Heventon, and enable me to pull together from those past decades as many as possible loose ends,

failed shreds and strands—
the unraveled threads and shards of my lives—
perhaps with the hope that
I could demonstrate how
the lore of my roles and
the lure of laurels,
rosy coma bouts
on copper tops and
copter-cop escort routs
had come about
and might be mostly finished,

and that, undiminished, I might be ready
for the heady Next Revelation-level
Ball.

All this is part of the miraculous, raucous and curious mosaic of my unfurling existence, as I contemplate it, worth the three-plus rebirths, the almost constant upward draw and warp, wrap and swirl of the spiral, and it fills me with joy to tears in these sublime waning but climbing days and years.

Thou Child of Joy,
Float round me, let me hear thy shouts,
thou happy
Shepherd-boy!

—S.T. Wordsmith

Getting a seat beside The Stranger *[probably across the aisle, as the narrow trimotor was configured with single seats on each side of the aisle. –Ed.]* out of Fresno was no problem this time.

So there we were, we two and ten more, as yet untested in what was to be our quest, strangely without a suggestion of apprehension or tension, as the blessed antique machine labored to take off and ascend.

As the drafty craft listed and entered its airy realm, the whine, clatter and shudder fore and aft were utterly overwhelming, for one of the three 12-piston engines was mounted bluntly on the nose of the ancient plane's grunting and shoddy aluminum body. But once we got aloft, the roar of the engines softened to a purr, then seemed to disappear as we wound and spiraled 'round and 'round ever higher into the thinning early-winter air.

I had correctly guessed that Dr. Robert T. had been in Berkeley to address a medical meeting of some sort where he said he'd given a short and fleeting report. He was, I learned ere long, the world's leading light and authority among those of that minority sorority *[sic –Ed.]* who study the relationship between health, diet and the size, shape and consistency of feculence, human and primate.

He told me he had been involved in coprology and scatomancy, and had theories about the correlations between the decline of civilizations and the absence of evidence of human coprolite matter in the jigs of archaeological digs. (But doesn't it quickly decay, I wondered?)

The lofty waft of soft stools and lost tools among exhausted gene pools of drooling fools?

In a more practical vein, he had also been arranging in Berkeley for the fabrication of an appliance similar to one commonly used for toasting, in a modification as a sun-fired shelf dryer to convert feces into boutique briquette pieces to burn in those chic alcove stoves he knew would be à la mode in remote abodes in the colder climes after the supplies of oil and gas declined, dried up and become scant and scarce, as he predicted, but he was far ahead of his time.

Also, the problem of rendering feces aseptic and odorless was never totally solved, and with new hepatitis strains, this problem was hardly negligible.

He and I hit it off slowly at first, until we discovered we were both from Heventon; then a belated latent and potent attraction came into action. Had our paths crossed before? Had we tossed in the baths? Was he The American Denim Dude on that *Gare de Grenoble* train platform in my student days in France?

In any case, though I hung on his every word, as we lumbered on through low-slung skies, I was near slumber, but then suddenly my mind flashed and latched onto a photo I had long before stashed away of "Phillip and Robert - '38" at YMCA summer camp near a Hopewell Indians site.

Yes, there as we plowed along among the flowing clouds I realized that this Robert I now call "B" and I had perhaps met more than 40 years before. I was taken back to that summer camp when I knew that certain unshirted Bob T. We were 12 or so, those delightful festive estival days and frightful nights among the ferns and wormy woods at Camp Kern, there by the

Mound Builders' Fort Ancient.

He already had a mature musculature and scarlet skin from the summer sun. His darker partner Phillip was an accomplished incipient classical pianist and organist, thin and tall, who bore the yoke and burden of having to practice his drab baroque notes every morning before day broke. And oddly it was Phillip for whom I did manifest a certain... something? because he seemed weaker? more feminine and accessible, less daunting, more like me, than Bob?

There had been, that summer, immature but not premature faintest stirrings of affection (love was a word that I had not understood; it was not spoken in our family) and pure though unsure sexual lure,

indeed unknown and thought-loathsome and wrong;
hot-slime lusty-youth same-sex duality,

but I was to evade it, afraid to really deal with any of it for a long decade and more. Although I could not have understood this dawning and spawning, I had been really drawn to Phillip and Robert. They were a pair aloof from the other sperm-caper swim-poofs and scam-ripe night-scare camper goofs, as I was as well, and proof was that the two balked at unpleasant scheduled sports and took secret walks into the woods to talk. They were to me magnetic, quiet, poetic and emphatically unathletic, and Phillip had a special arrangement that allowed him to practice for hours every day on an antique and out-of-tune piano in the big lodge and dodge the other awful hodgepodge of tough and regimented energetic stuff, exempt from the lame frenetically rough kinetic games we so detested and protested.

The first time we met, they invited me to go for a walk, and those photographs show our little clique in deep shade on a wooden bridge above the sweep of some rushing creek in a steep ravine of the lush primeval brush and forest green.

There was mystery about all this for me and I wanted to pursue the intriguing friendship with them after the strange days at camp, but my desire for brothers aborted in one short and troubled visit from the two of them to our shabby old house on Rookwood Street.

The duo was to come visit one fall day after a long trolley trek with transfer in the rain at Fifth and Main.

I recall those streetcars, that street, the crackling flash of wires above the tracks, and the pairs of unstable cables for the newer russet electric buses. I'd go downtown alone to the dime store or the Colonial Theater for vaudeville and magicians, the great Thurston's Horus-and-Tut magic act, or the slack-bone Great Blackstone.

Or in another version, not the trolleybus but a nervous mother waiting in the car as we tussled and wrestled, after all. My dusty attic-smelling bedroom an emphatic Kem-Tone blue.

No, that wasn't it. Was it Bob alone who came? No.
I made
Cool-aid.
Enough! I looked back for years and felt I'd been dealt
a rough loss in their rebuff, as they never came again.
So, as it turned out, the lad
named Robert I had
known that otherwise sad and depressing
prepubescent and incalescent summer stay
in the smelly and stressful YM bummer camp
was to emerge
and surge into my life
as my ruddy B
when I rediscovered him
as this great rubescent
rude-dude lover,
under-covers lewd and nude.

We had probably barely missed each other, a dozen or more years after the camp summer, in that Grenoble railroad station, it turned out, the *Gare de Grenoble....*

Parole et langue—when I heard these words from B's lips I knew he had at least a little knowledge of what some still called "philology," with its tesseract layers of vectors and matrices, and four-dimensional diachronic and synchronic tensions. Yes, he too had been in France at the *Université de Grenoble*, exactly a year after me, and had studied with Anton Duraffour and others I had known.

Yes, it perhaps *had* been B's tight bluejeans I saw on the Grenoble *Gare* platform, he arriving, I leaving for Heidelberg.

We drifted along now more softly, aloft in the Ford *Rubicon* Trimotor craft, and we were unaware and unprepared for presages of shift, long pilgrimages and voyages to strange islands and later African villages, as we lifted and slipped through the shrinking selvage of time.

The air had grown thin, and it seemed that we again listed a bit and were drowned in dreams.

The lotus magnet sling hits smog,
a Luna Mig-shot arrow
hangs latent, lag and slack,
high on the black lament of
harrowed slangs and hounds
unloosed from narrow bonds.
Hi! long-unmet time hiatus,
and you, slight and unfit tide.
* O Time, slant hug indeed,*
long-slung salient-hung
speeding steed,
in the ion hum and ohm-tugged light
of a Gestalt shuttle magi-hunt
hustling there in brightest night.

That film? *Lost Horizon!* Shangri-La! Where are we now? Sputter.

Did we ever land
as we somehow passed
on beyond Heventon

at last through some vast
and veiled celestial band
with a hushed
Theremin scream and wail?
  Time stood still, we thought,
but all the while,
stranded, we
rushed on,
caught up in a grand trap of
a love-and-life tidal dream
that happened in what seemed
but a momentary gap and lapse...
at Blennerhassett!

How many untolled years rolled past?

There was that time when shadow, trove and dream,
The dearth of common earthly lights,
  To me did seem
    Unfurled in perpetual dream,
The hoary moon, the flesh of night.
It is still now as it has been before —
  Turn wheresoe'er I may,
    By night or day,
      The things that I have seen I now can still adore

.

—S.T. Wordsmith

Chapter 17

Gaps

In what I call the Rubicon Gap: that weird lapsus,
the long sleep or dream there in New Blennerhassett,
those wrinkled decades
the wondrous floating Trimotor strained
to reach and rip through,
in what seemed the faded, shrunken shaved and devoured
shade of an hour, when The Worm wove in and out,
how many swept along, slept how long or
even stepped on through the seam, unwept?

For all of us dozens of Chosen Ones who flapped *["to flap,"*
a curious verb D uses for "to fly," perhaps from "flapero," the Nova Esperanto
term for a kind of airplane –Ed.] then or later into the lap of a Gap,
or found other ways to New Blennerhassett, there are a lot of
questions. Was the Blennerhassett compound, where Sarah and
others had already heeled in, the way on and up through the
dreamy stream to the stringy warm temporal fissure?
    Was it the port of entry into the Gap for all those who went?
And what about later Gaps, without the grim constraints of
Vonnegut's Timequake? *[Kurt Vonnegut, Jr., Timequake, 1997. –Ed.]*
    Perhaps ambrosial time in the Golden Ages
is "always" riddled and laced with frozen hollows and
tunnel spaces,

like a sponge, the germinal souls of new wormholes.
And such sojourns, turns and tortuous
time journeys, even when documented,
are viewed by some as merely demented
sunstroke syndromes, or worse.

And what about the lunacy of that earlier crazy Baron Blennerhassett's support of the much-slurred Aaron Burr Conspiracy, perhaps to break away from newly-formed USofA federacy.

Were we, as involuntary instruments in the creation of the new *Granda Konfedo* and the decentralization of Our Nation, about to emulate Burr's alleged and unproved deceit and sedition, and would we, like Burr, find defeat, dishonor and perdition?

What *is* certain, at least in this wry and splintered writer's view now in the subdued winter of life, is that something started to happen to the time contraption, and New Blennerhassett was one of the vortices, along with Serpent Mound and the Blue Hole, all in Ohio, as well as that funny place in my yard behind Spalding House in then-Los Angeles when I began all this research. And what of those later places in California (now Suda Kornukopio): PasaGlen, Burndale, Nomo Lake and the artificial Isle of St. Nola in the salty Slanto Sea. The problems we see throughout this work with years, chronology starting in the '80s, and even genealogy, attest to some such slippage.

Yet the Gaps were at once both seamless and separate eras,
somehow repeated, parsed and pasted,
speared and tapered.
And then erased.

Some who died on the tidal ride tried to live on,
and whole series of events seemed to be displaced or recur,
and collide there between the Old and the New Era,
in The Interspell, that hazy and skewed interstitial period
some called The Interstice or The Greek Years, *[also known as the "Alpha-Beta Years"—actually Alpha through Omega. —Ed.]*
perhaps itself a more general and widespread Gap?

I have tried to sort this all out, but all I can report is that although it was certainly not the first of the Gaps, the earliest I have personal evidence of began in the 1980s, sometime after the beginning of the AIDS epidemic, and I'm convinced that some of us were reborn in that early if not first Gap and tapped to live unnaturally long and rapt lives afterwards. Even then, in the early years of the truncated 21st Century, people commented that I looked so much younger than my chronological age. But that illusion too would fade.

Anyhow, it somehow got much later. (How easy that sounds!) And Sarah, after New Blennerhassett, however long she was there, was eventually ensconced not far from that finicky Ideth's new Merganser headquarters in the pinnacle of the old Chrysler Building, helping direct the erection of her New Mews-Manhattan Emerald Gardens Project and, still none-too-humble, claiming that she herself had stumbled onto a rough-and-tumble unencumbered "Transfinite Number Cause" for that earthly pause, the Gap or Gaps we few had gone through.

In any case, in my more simple and subdued view, I believe that, though dates and years—now lost in the cataclysmic and miasmal chaos of scrambled recorded knowledge—along with rhythms, births, sexuality shifts, rebirths, non-deaths, "Transitions" and so on, used to be important, and could be counted, numbered, duplicated, remembered, reproduced, re-created, listed and glossed in earlier times, events now are but a spiral pulsar ritual pillar and rite-addled and catapultic plurality slog, plying and ripping through the lace of time as a gluey binder, a Divine End-dive into the hot and holy toe-to-heel white leaves of three-ring hubbub, The Blue Hole Gap. The *Witlof* Factor.

Yes, repetition manifests as manifold coincidences, and that is how It All Came Down.

The slack hunt hangs, now and again, stagnant, caught in some gasbag brig awaiting the Turn of the Wheel, when grinding gears and raging shifts do then indeed stay it all and relink ghostly years.

If every cog had a different size and shape... Bang! Cock!
Every dog [*god? –Ed.*] its day, its clock, Gads!

The Very Idea of Multiplication! Too much stuff!

Time fortunately prevents everything from happening at
once.

Indeed, the sublime twisting spiral of phantom Rhythm
and fleeting Rhyme together—those synchronizing diachronic
collapse-me-back crunchers—impel me ahead yet a spell and

hold It All

fairly well a-tether !

Yes, we do hang and hug on a slick cant, a slippery slant.

Chapter 18
A Peaceful Dénouement

Ideth and Sarah had long been united in solidarity and allied in their basic biased political philosophies. And they foresaw with some clarity, they thought, the veritably debasing trends that would bend the United States and overtake it in the end unless the powerful negative fe'ral forces could be dismantled or rechanneled.

After Sarah left New Blennerhassett and joined Ideth in that eerie, weird and now-become weary Chrysler Building eyrie, Ideth, the titular head and sire *[sic –Ed.]* of the now-long-matriarchal Merganser empire, perhaps like Wem before, went into some sort of pseudo-"Transition" by staging several fake death capers to remove herself from the scene and covertly oversee from afar her successor Sarah in her lair high up there in her tower. Warily at first, but primarily secure in the notion of Sarah's devotion to her scheming, dreams and visions, the berserk and quirky work of generations, Ideth thus disappeared voluntarily from active participation, leaving Sarah, as we have said, there in the icy green upper reaches of that art deco skyscraper spire in the Vonnegut Memorial Harp Museum she had always dreamt of establishing and inhabiting.

Until her final, more natural "Transition" might take her "over," unfettered Across the River, so to speak, Ideth moved quietly to PasaGlen, near Angelus Eden, and started seeing artist

Andrew Gorgon, who was inspired by Santa Teresa de la Cruz's *Castillo Interior* to build Ideth an *Interna Kastelo* that she called, stretching a point, her "Heaven Castle." Here, in the last secluded few years of her life, Ideth shrewdly had a nice idyllic time of it. These last butch years would make a fascinating book, for she apparently took on the look of what she thought to be a sort of innate soulmate, Idasora Phyphe Nutcan, and set out to emulate and carry on the life of that great creative choreographic star of over a century earlier. So, at an advanced age she took up the dance and glided about entranced and with amazingly enhanced ductile ability, masculinity and agility. She owed her second youth and new romance, she said, to the use of that remarkable but long discredited chemical juice, dimethyl sulfoxide (DMSO)—actually a byproduct in the manufacture of paper—whose uses were discovered by my Grandfather George Ludwig at the MEWS in the early '20s.

But alas, there still was no singly rigorous or vigorous potential world figure or rapper of stature, no bigger digger or trigger finger who espoused Ideth and Sarah's goals, and the public was never much aware of those three rarely-seen Washington queens, the Jesterson Trio. Ideth had apparently never developed any affection for her roster of foster "sons," Thom and Wilmar, not even Jack, but I gather she came to see them as instruments, if imperfect, of her Grand Design, and they did in the end, especially under Sarah, manage in all their obscene, obscure and secret bumbling behind the scenes to bring about bizarre legislative changes and hence abet the discrediting and eventual rupture and dissolution of the federal structure, before they disappeared into even more complete oblivion while the grander forces and notions set in motion took over and raced to change the thrust and face of history, for what Sarah had dubbed "the Final Dissolution."

The earlier unwary, probably unwise and scary reliance by Ideth and even Sarah on the soft Thom Jestersons *[sic –Ed.]* to carry forward their own lofty ideals, seemed to be a bad draw and the potential flaw in the whole supreme scheme, as these three yawed off course and relied too much on sly and oft idle, dull and soft-loaded federal government lay-oafs and daft and fay lily-pawn dolts they designated to help behind the scenes in Congress. Yes, their cohorts were finally like a dose of lye in the eye, vandalizing everything along the way, most in the end scandalized, some even dead to the world they thought they were daringly and unsparingly preparing.

The flair for greater and more traitorous
thought-surefire political ventures
that ended in infamous failures—
including fatal-fuse-behavior and false-flare liar plans
launched by the laissez-faire Jesterson clan
and the various often notorious amorous affaires
of Thom, Wilmar and Jack Taffeta,
beginning with the Canal Lad Scandal,
the sad suicide of a purportedly unclad
capital DC-anal cad, the possibly false reports
of Thom's own suicides, plus
the attendant early thwarted, insurmountable
and aborted attempts to
get him elected to Congress—
yes, all this, led rather directly,
(in my somewhat detached view)
to the ultimately even more covert directions
the matchless Sarah and
the covert Blennerhassett faction
took to scratch, hatchet,
and abandon inane
political campaigns, actions
and candidates altogether,
and go on to forge a new and more devious path;
and the Jesterson Trio to eventually
proceed with minor subversions
which did, in a sense,

to a limited extent,
help undermine
at this dire juncture
the entire Fe'ral Government structure.
The Jesterson antics were often
a stressful mess and laughable debacle,
for example, when at long last the
harassed-but-unsurpassedly daring
Thom Team arrived one Halloween
by proverbial Green Submarine
to take over the Patriot Machine behind the scenes.

But although this failed, the mincing Jack Taffeta actually did, Sarah unconvincingly said, find a way under the White House roof and even into a Presidential bed, though this invasion was destined to be but clandestine. But she claimed he came by intimate information that helped foment further rifts and chasms in the corrupt Administration, and bring about the overdue rout of those terminally weakened, blackened, nasty, mistaken and drunken louts

of the disloyal idiot "Beacon of Democracy" lot,
for church-deacon dogmas started to fall like palm
frond fans,
and soon enough,
with certain rather McLuhanesque notions,
Sarah did eventually set forces in motion
to bring about the final disgrace, firing, arrest and replacement
of the Elder Dynasty Faces, and the decentralization
and dissolution of the government
to try to transcend ghastly and grotesque
losses and disasters just before The Interspell.

What finally succeeded was a bizarre scheme to use illicit means to tilt the election against that pedestrian, inertial, embedded Presidential Dynasty that was so heavily backed by the viral industrial-military consortium, and when the election was declared rigged, a deal was somehow sealed to appoint as President a mildly charismatic and somewhat laconic but eager movie-actor-become-preacher—from the South—who was furtively dedicated to the dismemberment of the Fe'ral Government.

Had this coup been less-than-adroitly carried out—largely by Sarah herself, though the Trio played a role as well—it could well have led to insurrection and revolution. But the masses were catatonic and weary and had lost faith in the government to do anything right after wearing years of fateful wars and natural and environmental catastrophe, bloodily suppressed class battles and famine. And miraculously, the people went along with the new President, approved the *Supera Ĉarto* and a transition to the *Granda Confedo,* as planned by the *Supera Konfabo* (Great Conference), that was called in Venice by Sarah and that Hakem van Funk we're about to meet. So, miraculously, a peaceful dénouement resulted, and it all worked out in the end for our imperfect heroes, though they never laid claim to fame. But more about all that anon.

Why not Sarah as leader, the reader may ask. By design she had remained unknown and her past was so badly scratched and patched that she wouldn't have had a chance, and anyway the masses were still not ready for another female leader, though a gynocracy of sorts was fortunately to come about shortly.

It was not to be until the high-pitched cries of the Dixie Trixi Revelations and Emanations that an undefied and undisguised True Leader was surprisingly to arise, succeed and be heeded by the formerly headless masses. This happened in Suda Kornukopio on Sarah's Isle of St. Nola in the salty Slanto Sea there beyond Hemet; and over in Dresden with Carson Proust and Kurt Bonplaisir.

Those of us on that Ford *Rubicon* who went through what Sarah told me not long ago was the "FuQ'u" or Fantum Q'um *[perhaps akin to "Quantum Foam"? —Ed.]* on the way to Blennerhassett seemed to operate in a different overlay dimension, floating above all that happened, like the Auracrucians that we were, waiting to fulfill our ultimate roles while the unsparing apoplectic cataclysms of tide and time prepared the New Era. And the rest of the world was deep asleep in another way, complacent and slipping swiftly into that much-heralded but deceptively fragile, imperiled and brief New Millennium, which all too quickly led to those multiple monofocal local wars, ignoble terrorism and the equally dishonorable battle against it, so-called "globalization," and the Silicon Cocoa Rift and all it foreshadowed, straddled there on the proscenium of the false-start 20th century.

On a global scale, The Will to Go On was gone, everything tilted on stilts in the seething silt of the hot rising seas or wilted and melted in the heat, and was but half rebuilt; and Old Europe came briefly apart under that Dresden Fezdom lot and the earth was ravaged and savaged in the spoil and famine turmoil of those damned Oil War years. But at last, after perhaps the worst decades in history, the Final Chaos was narrowly averted when the Supera Ĉarto was accepted in much of the world.

I've recounted what happened in Nova Washingtono, but I only wish I knew how that miracle came about in the rest of the world. If only I could reminisce, tell it better and fill in the missing letters, but I recall only that we made it through the blessed mist, muss, muddle and befuddling mess of those years to and through The Interspell.

I'm sure I had some global role in all this
and witnessed some of it
as we approached the Grand Goal,
but it must have been during a Gap, or some kind of "hole."
I have tried to approach it on a personal basis
and at least find out something about
what I myself contributed,
through Sarah's super-secret CenterPersFiles,

but she has, alas—perhaps
(I am sure she would lamely, shamelessly
and blamelessly claim)
in an attempt
to "protect my name" and
de-scent the content—
deleted, hidden or circumvented
with guile any reference to me
in the Mobi-Fone and Wander-bust tracer files
at CenterNet.
I had been relying on these sources
for help in my quest, to round out
this present monumental document,
but was distressed
when my request was rejected
and I learned that Sarah's
best-intent tampering
with historical records
extended even to my own long-pampered
but now totally unattested LifeFile.

I was Erased!

Chapter 19
Africa

B

Through that Rubicon Gap and on beyond, until his "Transition," through the "Pharaoh Hole," B, this medical researcher and foremost authority on coprology in the world, was to be my friend and sometime companion and lover.

B was a curious doctor of procto-osteopathy and serious scientist of the Edison ilk, and as a coprologist he pioneered the promising premise that most weaknesses and diseases could be diagnosed by a combination of what some detractors called divination—actually, examination of the feces and related matters and factors, not an easy thesis and one that perturbed, displeased and disturbed a legion of sullen Viennese colleagues of the mind-healer persuasion.

At my behest, B pledged to later do cutting-edge research abutting on and in pursuit of my own mystical both conical and vortical umbilical sensations. The reader will recall that I had that bizarre condition, the so-called U-Burn, though my case was not as "salient" as that of Wilmar Scheedick, Man Draake and others.

But B was not quick enough on the fast-draw, as they say, and, alas, though it was decades later, he passed on too soon, that afternoon on his way to an isle in the Nile, and it would have to be in that swirling Next Whirl, I then thought, that he got around to the omphalos, up there beyond the wild blue altostratus, etc.

I sometimes speculated in jest that if he didn't hasten to complete his projects Down Here, he would have to import loads of raw material he needed for his fecal studies Up There, past the Evil Veil via some murky, milky inter-cosmic or mega-lactic meta-galactic, infra-colonic oooom-phallic freight train, funneled through the bunghole tunnels of unfurling, foiling time.

No, in that nice rhapsodic Rapper Paradise on the brighter side of The Divide, that "New Place," as the Dixie Trixi followers and others are calling it now, there may well be no "raw material" at all as we know it for scatological or even omphalic research—no beings, no beans, no idyllic umbilical buttons discernibly jutting or butting and bursting out, or in. One of B's abiding concerns, he suggested sometimes, was that such research might not be needed in that borough of the Truly-New Whorl.

In fun, did you infundibulum, wid yer, um, calla thallus, Blum? Joyless callus-voice of Bloom and Doom? Re-Joyce!

I suspect it is indeed the umbilicus that is the magnetic gamete and net-center of the body, the area where we sense magnetism as well as gravity to fuel our other proclivities and depravities—the Relativity Cavity, where those two forces come together and either mesh or clash, our own private hole in the fence.

Sexual penetration of, or by, the umbilicus is somewhat rare, as sexual ingressive divergences go, but it is to be expected that those geosurgeon nurses who are already snipping out penises for womb-men have not been slow in showing the path. —Vidi-World Web

Eb

Well before Ebenezer Grogan was my lover
in Venice, California, for a year or more,
he had become a Qabbalist,

following his loony saloon days
in a San Francisco commune
in the hippy days of "The Haight" enclave,
where he lived with a tight gay group
involved in sometimes tragic drug heights
and flurries of both
black- and white-magic furies;
and some of these went on, as did he,
to be active socially and politically,
for he soon surmounted and buried
his hash delusions
and went into seclusion
on a mountaintop, sobered,
and started over
with his Qabbala quest
and All The Rest.
It is Ebenezer's work,
frontier research
and "queer spirit"
that concern us here.
Eb had become interested in decrypting
and unzipping the mysteries
of the Great Egyptian Pyramids,
and it was then that I met him
and we did what we did
amid talk of The Holy Grid.
I must warn that I am sworn
to an icy secrecy policy
about Eb's current faery theories,
but I *can* say that for a few years he
was enraptured
on the forefront and leading edge
of magnetism and gravity studies,
especially what he called "pure rapture forces"
—perhaps localized gravity reductions—

that could be conjured, lured or captured for cures
and, what's even more sure,
for massive heavy lifting and even levitation
—which could be one explanation
for the Pyramid erection mystery.
I shall refer to these
here and in future mentions
as the occult form
of that Holy Grid,
what Eb called
the Gravity-Delta tensions,
or the G-D Force.
Eb's theory had to do with, and I quote:

"...stunning and fleet triangular (Delta) gravity sheets of the Substance G, made up of strings or strands which fan out from the Sun and can be described, abstractly, as two-dimensional rays, infinite in number; figures defined by a single point of emanation and the farthest points on the surface they strike.

"This two-dimensional G-D Force exists in the Third [sic –Ed.] Dimension, Time, and through its temporal emanation operation it acquires a Fourth Dimensional 'thickness' property, or perhaps it gains 'substance' in terms of Finity = Infinity."

When I try to get Eb to clarify this, he refuses, won't discuss it and simply fusses a bit and says, somewhat incongruously, "Maybe they had some sort of air hammers."

Yes, he believed those bewildering guild masters—the Pyramid Builders—were able to use the Gravity-Delta rays in splendid and now-fabled ways to attenuate the force of gravity, either locally or globally.

Of course no evidence or proof of this force has been found, and perhaps some sort of "air hammers" were actually conjured up by the ancient Egyptian priests through dances and trances. And, if they were indeed 30 or even only 12 feet tall, as some have surmised, their cants and chants would have been mighty surprising rustles and rumbles indeed.

Or perhaps they could summon up the whole alternative or superimposed hunk of the universe in a minuscule chunk to create from *negative matter* various kinds of tools that used the forces of air and gravity, invisible to mortal man.

Although Eb kept his strange notions about gravity to himself and thus avoided ridicule, he had conjectured that it was "localizably variable and harnessable," a concept that has gurged and resurged into prominence much later.

Simply put, according to Eb's bold theory, gravity is our most immediate experience of the cosmic-force energy sources in their physical manifestation.

The Pharaonic Village

[There are unresolved chronology problems in this journal-type section, with related fragments apparently written during—and concerning—various periods. —Ed.]

And my love B's search for human droppings and traces deep in outback South Africa has whisked him and C *[The rôle of C in D's later life is unclear in his writings, and we learn little about him or the relationship —Ed.]* —not without some risk—away from me during this Northwestern Tetartosphere winter mist, so bitter this year, and though I stay here in Holywood in the warmth of Suda Kornukopio, there is a coldness in my worn old bones and a whimper in my heart that cries out for *human* warmth.

[And perhaps a little later. —Ed.]

Alas, B and C are gone on then to a South African autumn international forum in this our lingering spring *[The apparent confusion of seasons can be attributed to the Southern Hemisphere shift. —Ed.]*; B also to do some muddy study there, the pursuit of minute base and trace minerals that lace the stones around some parts of the old Raymond Dart diggings—those minerals that evidence "turd chemistry," that is, as I put it (to B's mock horror). It all seems far-fetched to me, but then the scientist must leave no stool unturned, toad unstoned or turd unsung, so to speak.

And C will translate for B and do his Bantu linguistic studies.

I may join them there, despite my dislike of Africa, now so decimated.

My own tool *[probably "stool," but then, perhaps not. —Ed.]*, by the way, is healthy by B's standards as well as my own, as long as I eat well and properly, though C would not agree.

[Then much later, further north —Ed.]

We were in West Africa together, B and C and I, at the time. They were there on their latest obsessed quests, which they curiously claimed overlapped and even coalesced. We had just come into Ouagadougou from a deserted desert village when B fell violently ill.

B knew that his stressful decades in equatorial Africa might one day catch up with him in the form of some health crisis or one of those detested pests, so omnipresent on that continent.

At first he thought it was "just" Coxsackie virus, but soon the iridescent iris-halo symptom of the Trans-Val Lily-virus appeared, and the diagnosis was clear.

Instead of returning on the next flight to Paris or Angelus Eden, he insisted on going by Chiron Autogyro to Cairo, where Eb was ironically now practicing with some success his loosely dodecaphonic acoustic healing techniques under a grant from, and in a space provided by, that now-grown-vast Egyptian theme park and think tank, The Pharaonic Village, on a new man-made isle in the Nile, surreptitiously funded by Sarah, at my behest.

Here Eb had been recognized for his scientific research and given a bountiful suite of rooms near a reproduction of Tutankhamun's tomb, reconstructed here in Cairo as unmartyred and uncursed Howard Carter had found it in the 1920s.

For Eb, The Pharaonic Village had also brought the blackest basalt and constructed a replica of what he claimed were the "acoustic healing vaults," those little-commented and still-quite-encumbered dead-ends off the entrance tunnel in one of the colossal Great Giza Pyramids.

But so swift was the onset of the final crazed phases of what had perhaps been an older long-smoldering disease, that B collapsed in the back of a taxi (Eb had wanted to try to send an ambulance to the airport) and by the time we reached Eb's Project Two enclave at Pharaonic Village, B had apparently felt he could not be saved and had self-administered a sinister cantharis cathartic, injecting himself with a gross and apparently lethal dose of something that brought him a quick and extremely serene "Transition," but to me it was grossly morose.

Eb nonetheless took great pains to carry B's remains into his reproduced Sound Chamber, dubbed Pharaohs Portal, to remain there for a few days before a strange burial he arranged in the shallow sand not far from the Great Pyramids.

And it was in this same chamber but days later that Eb subjected me and C to the "Pharaoh's Arrow," as he called it, a thrilling healing rite, enhanced with a course of milky tonic lactose brews amid the echoes and galactic forces of Eb's acoustic pyramid chamber.

I was not surprised some years later when Eb called me to say that B had somehow arisen and reappeared one day from his dry tomb there in the Nile Valley, pure and surely cured, and that the two of them would meet us in Angelus.

But, in what I considered a terrible anticlimax, he soon disappeared, to my deep grief and disappointment.

Chapter 20

History

Looking back now, the so-called "Communist Threat" and the "Cold War" that obsessed a generation of the 20th century are hardly remembered. All those years ago there had been no empirical reason to hope for the sudden political miracle: the decline of the feared, treacherous, murderous and ominous Communist Universe, but it did finally whirl and hurl to earthly dust.

And it seemed equally remote that an end would ever come to the later "Terrorism Threat" embodied in the aftermath at the beginning of the century of that Manhattan "dual shaft disaster," and even worse, what followed, with the ache of chaos over much of the hot, quaking globe, with Brother against Brother and One against the Other; near total—not merely subtle or anecdotal—atmospheric and oceanic depletion and unprecedented fury, tempest, fear and panic; the very Cradle of It All rocked to Babylonian dust; the bloodiest imaginable battles between United IranIraq East and SaudIsrael; the diseases that decimated Africa and half of Asia; and on our own shores of glee of yore, corpses of the poor and the forces of gore from rising sea to parched and shimmering lea.

But finally, unexpectedly, as often happens, perhaps through sheer exhaustion, history revealed its hand and the wars did end.

We saw the dissolution and fall of that arsenic era malicious Satan's Nest minority Muslim offshoot and reemergence of the respectable Islamic strain; terrorist enclaves brought to their knees; peace across the world; and for better or worse, the collapse of eros-scarred Rome's Holy Seat and the Highly Exalted Pompacy, as it had come to be known, split ass-under; as well as the breaking up and taming of the Great Nations, including the USofA.

And this was all accompanied by that incredible Pitti Treaty and the *Supera Ĉarto*, the "Great Charter," that led one winter to splinter the remnants of the Great Nations into multiple weak *konfedoy* and *sosovoy* (loose confederations) and the creation in North America of that super-loose solution that was to be the *Granda Konfedo,* alongside its north and southwest sisters Kanfedo and Aztlanafedo.

Although the nuclear provisions of this *Supera Ĉarto* were somewhat unclear, it did court support among the long-shorted and enfeebled peoples of a world that was now without a Pop, as His Elegance had come to be called, and it aimed to save the race from facing disgrace and basic destructive effacement by vaulting away nuclear weapons of assault and halting their manufacture, though it did not quite rout the faulty genetic restructuring that had come about.

Some have advanced the thesis that we would have gone on to further awful, unpredictable, unlawful and divergent demoniacal misdeeds, with the evolution of the human race drifting away from its current or any other awesome Divine Solution, if Sarah Spiderman Siegfried had not created Magi-Net and the other new "nets" and gained control over the whole main communication and information grid, as she did, thus enabling her to dominate, manipulate and contaminate the "data" in the so-called Omnibus Beta Databases on the Vidi-World Web, with the resultant fortunate thwarting of scientific research in general and nuclear development and weapon proliferation in particular, as well as hampering or reversing the perverse genetic duplication and gene restructuring, so there was no further rupturing and tampering with the secrets and mysteries of the universe.

Starting some years before The Interspell, major "Print Media Providers," as publishers were then called, in an attempt to foster some vague New Order, gave considerable attention to the old Internet and various paperless book forms, and it now appears that Heliofoil, developed at the MEWS, may well be of importance.

Early on, Sarah had approached SPEPNET (the Small Press Editors and Publishers Network) and the Literature Program of FEPOFART (that old Federal Endowment for the Preservation of the Arts), for both of which I was then an advisor, in what I now believe was an unforgivable surreptitious plot to blot and wipe them all out. Together we devised *ElectroMag,* an electronic network that was to lure all the surviving "independent" still-paper printers, presses and publishers and become the sole hub for disseminating creative writing by (and for) the "privileged few," the so-called PaPoets (Paper Poets) or ElectroScribes, utilizing all the "latest" technology, which was, alas, soon to become unavailable to the general masses.

Yes, *ElectroMag,* published out of the SPEPNET offices at Retrococo Foundation in Venice, was to be our
odd love-nod and punt
to the braver cod-rod and mod-squad
underground democracy pod that favored
saving "freedom of preach, teach and speech."
This new *ElectroMag* was made available on a special limited ElectroNet, which allowed access to almost all the writing by the steroid-bereft left-side-riot editors of the remaining hundreds of SPEPNET magazines, but to what avail?

No, I didn't realize I'd been duped as part of the Grand Plan, and I was terribly disappointed when this venture failed—for lack of "users."

But it did leave room for the later *MagRap* and the more

vital live performance art boom of the strictly oral RaPoets (also known as HipHoPoets) we now see on every street corner and doorstep, the New Era troubadours. It is to be hoped that once things settle down again there can be some amalgamation of the old written forms with the newer oral ones.

A seminal function and sadly the only lasting contribution of this ElectroNet was its dissemination of information about and convocation of the *Supera Konfabo,* that so-called "Big Conference" of the Decemviri, conceived and led by Hakem von Funk at Retrococo in the Old Venice City Hall.

I had met Hakem, then known as Hal, in the early 1970s when he helped me promote that magazine I had founded, *Beyond Cismontane Review,* and guided the establishment of Retrococo Foundation.

Von Funk had been sent to the Middle East
on a '60s business mission about which
he had sincere doubts,
but these were soon mingled
with his singular obsession
with some Muslim sphere chiefs—
and especially the young princes—
he came to revere
and not long after,
he told me with a smirk,
that he was to work
with the famed, shameless and berserk
leader of a great
unnamed Arab state.
He had fallen in love
more from afar
than he would have liked,
I'm sure,
with this bizarre and insecure sinecure,
a not-so-pure young Arab royal,
a kid, a disloyal prince-in-line,

who tore around unfettered
in his fine, fast and fur-lined
pink convertible,
that blasted out terrible old
AmArabian rock-n-roll.
But then Hakem, always covert,
went out of sight
for a few obscure years
in what appears to have been
a Blennerhassett Gap,
then reappeared
—perhaps guided by Sarah—
as a sublime and wiser
prime advisor on the Arab World
to that terrible, troubled,
slow-reader sheep twin
early-21st-century
dynasty leader
dubbed Double Ewe
(but dumber than Dolly),
that sleepy Bo-peep-follower creep,
yes, you've guessed it,
that boring burning brush
who tried to mash and crush
the Fertile Crescent
and caused such unprecedented
loss and chaos.
But all the while
von Funk was secretly
still in cahoots
and, all smiles, conspiring
with clever new offshoots
of several Arab empires,
until he was discovered
and fired by that inept President.

So Hakem returned to the Middle East
to become a Muslim elder, and
who could have guessed that
some decades later, at the behest
of this western guest von Funk,
the swimmer sheik al-Hambra Ta'rif,
at best a mincing, unconvincing and aging punk,
was to come to rest as head and Emir of the dread
Dresden Fezdom fiefdom and thiefdom
after a big chunk of Europe fell to the East.
But then, von Funk,
in his luscious and frilly mullah robes,
there on the other side of the globe,
had a change of heart, when he met Carson and Kurt
there in Dresden
—and eventually Dixie Trixi—
and was drawn and fascinated
by the limitless possibilities created
by their new ecumenical movement.
I have little doubt that he correctly envisioned
warring nations finally brought to their knees
along with a new "spiritual dawning"
all over the globe caused in part by
that total oil shutdown,
fadeout, rout and bout,
in which he was not uninvolved,
to say the least.
So Hakem's original plot was not
to come about, and he was later to turn tail
in a sense, and be hailed
for his humanitarian and peace efforts,
and for actually freeing Europe
from the Dresden Fezdom he'd once fostered.
And he finally became the head
of the Decemviris that led to the

Supera Ĉarto.

As for Sarah, she had long put up with Hakem, because she knew that any unrest or stir of the international stew would further her goals at least, and some even thought she might herself have been behind Hakem's wily surreptitious and shifting activities.

And as, perhaps, must come to pass
in some periods of cataclysmic collapse,
some who had "vision" were riven
from pretense and material descents,
and given a high mission by unexpected events,
and though at times seeming reckless,
or even demented, abstruse,
indirect or subversive,
they had honest and pure goals
and overriding self-control as they
totally disregarded reason and personal gain
and used and extolled
more plain power for good
in the crucial old
political and social sense
than could have happened
at almost any other time
in the memory of man.
All this is to be coupled, I hope,
though not soon enough, I'm sure,
with the amazing revelation
(as in the days of the crazy raising
of the myriad Great Egyptian Pyramids,
which probably also involved
a skillful tampering with the tilting earth's
evolving magnetic cavity and kinetic field)
of the probably inadvertent, convergent

slight weakening or taming, as the case may be,
of gravity! And this reduction
of the natural force
and thus the weight of all earthly matter
(an astounding second time around)
might lead to hyper-productive machinery
and energy conservation tools
to energize and "etherealize" the earth
and lead to the birth of an idyllic new jewel,
a whirling pearly and potentially perfect world.

The initial interstitial Year Alpha began the crucial and essential Interspell period, that grand unplanned slant-tug back-hoe black-hole limbo chaos in the limelight-climb to a blissfully chiming rhyme zone and harmonizing time that dragged on so very long.

Yes, all this led to
mending the blend,
fending off the down-trend,
winding up the soft end,
and finally responding to the no longer waning
underlying attendant social and spiritual concerns
and the founding and molding of the foundling *konfedoy*.
And down spin the glare-spangled
under-gangs of the twilight-gods march
into the marshes.
Peace!

So, that stressed Dresden, after rising out of communist shambles, and then briefly becoming a European capital—a fire storm again on the forest rim under a fezdom chief—finally redressed and was to be the seat of an ecumenical revolution under ageless Kurt Bonplaisir and Carson Proust, still there, as I said, now clad in parasilk nunnery drag, waiting to join the later Dixie Trixi movement we will soon enough meet.

But now, on to other matters.

Chapter 21

Mars

LIFE FOUND ON MARS!

The speed of light is not constant.

Black holes give up their secrets!

The slant hug o' time cants.

La loi de la pesanteur n'est plus vraie.

Amoeba possible in meteoric rock.

Chapter 22

St. Em

It was before B and the Rubicon Gap that my then-lover
M was diagnosed with AIDS.
For five fiery live-and-jive fury years,
before *It,*
there were sweaty warning signs
of the drum bing-and-bang
fevered ringing clang beginning:
already the rash appeared,
the hotdog gas inside,
the pop-ion rod ignited and the absurd
obscured brewing infection appeared.
Curious and confusing cosmos music
outcropped and, coppered,
crept copious and promiscuous
into the porous corpus orifices;
followed, then, by poor mucous and sour scum
spinning there under the thin skin
as saddest apple-ass sagged,
weighed down and downy-gonad-conned,
as a new nib grew reb,
and a rib grinned through.
The Diagnosis: Giant Dose,
a cold iron bout

with the Viral Load.
Yes, Adios the fiery
angel ballade façade.
Yes, for my doubting lamb:
Over and Out
(of the fray and the
violent tin-pan AIDS tympany of
John Paul Corigliano's
first thundering symphony).

Then later, that two-faced AIDS
perhaps sprouted ALFA-ACE
(AIDS-like Fluid- and Air-Carried Enterovirus),
and both persisted and resisted
at least in part because drugs had been found
that soon abounded, to help victims "maintain"
and they attained deceptive complaisance;
and also an imperfect vaccine
had been proclaimed,
but mainly against some older strains.
In the end, all this bred mutated new stuff
and provoked a malicious alphabet salad of
other illnesses and maladies
new to the race, unfurling
for the world to face.

   But the next stop for M: all-knowing gnosis,
metamorphosis and higher tidings
—count the noses.
"But he lived on?" you ask,
"and survived these diseases?"
like those other Jeezes?
in palingenesis?
What I know is,
as I write here from this great distance in time,

my beloved M,
dwelled somewhere There,
perhaps in his own Gap,
waiting until the moment
of fomentation came,
there in the heather
near the Healing Camp dell
at Deep Pit, New Jersey
where so much that was so hopeful
was coming to rest,
although we still are not apace or abreast
in this Great Scourge-curing race
and do not know the sure outcome,
in this mighty test,
much less the quelling and purging
of its sequel's still-hidden source.

Beloved artist and martyr, the saintliest of unstained painter-Saints-To-Be, gentle and so lovingly cuprous, later known as Brother M, and finally now St. Em, he was to become part of the triumviri, with Kurt Bonplaisir and Carson Proust, that went to bat on the pastoral lap in the palatial Cativan temple apse and unsat and catapulted the last lapsed Cataleptic Pop and, starting with some of the more jetset Jute-suits, the Catamitic Orders and the Bed-a-nic-teen Debs, assured the transformation of the wary and querulous old pedophile Orders, from their contradictory sham-tam clerestories and promontories into newly mystical schools of high altruistic and spiritual vision, berets and all, down there in the alleys.

Those merry Healing Camps
that not-quite-departed Brother M
returned to start after his personal Gap,
around the airy Deep Pit Uranium-gravel
quarry, grew and expanded and it does seem
that the sick were prone
to stay alive and thrive

if they did the daily
Schlepp-'n'-Jive trek
and the Dread Zeppelin
live Moiseyev Mersey Beat
down the neat and steep
uranium slopes and stopped past
the U-dope core deposit hit,
that fine but weak
main-frame refrain of the
uranium strata
my uncle Nemuel Hamilton had earlier come
to find and claim and hoped to refine.
It was my Uncle Nemuel,
the inventor on my father's side,
who fortuitously discovered
that lustrous metallic element
under the ground in the Jersey Deep Pit,
a thin earth vein of the rare Uranium,
though it was dilute and too impure
to mine
but he continued looking for a better strain
only to ironically slacken,
stumble and crumble,
gasp and clasp his throat,
fall back in his tracks
startled and smarting with a fatal heart attack.

Unfortunately, there had also ensued,
      preying on the sick and defenseless,
      an endless series of slick upstart
      supraritual upstairs lurer quacks
who began in those years to join
in the race for an off-beat cure
for AIDS, ALFA-ACE
and some of the cancers.

And these rival pseudo-spiritual father-confusers
rattled off spirals of stupor and baffling "answers"
and muddled prattle that befuddled
and coddled the victims
with crazy dictums and nostrums.
And this was not dispelled even into The Interspell,
    for there was still a proliferation of hearse-chase
pump-us parsons
and wrathful and pompous pseudowraith preachers
on the rostrums of heretical faiths,
campy sonar jump-arse healers
and heyday oasis savior-teachers
spieling about Hades-aversion behavior.
And, despite all Sarah's better efforts—
this was not to get sorted out and suppressed
until Brother M assumed his post-Cativan chair,
and that young Stephen,
stiffened his faith,
and later became St. Ephen.

Stephen, St. Ephen, a guy I may have met earlier in a YMCA room, perhaps Cousin Alice's lost nephew, recurs in every pimple-face: Trenton hovels, classes I teach and taught, even bars in strange cities. Every Steve, Steven or Steffen is my lost kin, as is every World War airman my lost youth, like Carson Proust and Kurt Bonplaisir, cruising in their Dresden silk and leather, together, birds of a feather. Ironically, Stephen was among the first to contract ALFA-ACE.

Yes, Stephen
fastened his sheath,
shook his spear,
tapped past,
spat out what he knew
and joined the new spiritual crew.

And these incipient saints of a new healing order were to be part of a universal movement that would ultimately find voice in the bizarre "Dixie Trixi Revelations and Emanations."

The message that came in these Emanations, disseminated through Audinet and Radnet as well as Magi-Net that by then permeated the globe, and even on our own Vortexanet, was not a totally new one, and it was loaded with an essential ecumenical element mixed with pseudoscientific esoteric gibberish to attract the crass masses, but the message of tolerance and acceptance was new and it was perhaps a true re-creation and re-emergence of the spiritual hurly-burly that had arisen millennia earlier and lasted, but became so twisted, varied and buried in the insistent doggerel verse and list-and-lurch of those various old church dogmas, the latter-day fanaticism of frenetic phratries, some misguided followers of what Trixi called "the two Mo's" (Moses and Mohammad) and other lesser leaders, Jesus pretenders, hysterical anti-cross hypothesis teasers, historical synthesis teachers, and johnny-come-latelies and -belatedlies from Genesis to Croesus, or whatever.

Indeed, the world was ready to listen to *anything.*

Lash the wheel, wash the heel. All's well, eh?

Chapter 23

Time

But enough of my ramblings and foreshadowing jumps. In my old age I do trumpet and tramp around so, at times. In these tortuous labyrinthine matters I think it best to lump together things as they come into my head, and sum up and direct my own sometimes confusing bedtime musings and interpretations to the task at hand. I need to let the conflicting "data" and ostensible facts just stand pat.

My theory: The Ink of History is but murky blots, while mythical iconic and fictional stories and mysteries knot together and sort themselves out in future years from myriad short airy and rimy Corinthian versions, Ionic and iambic verses, relaxed Doric syntax, ironic tellings, and inverted spellings. *[We have left this passage more or less intact, if only to make the reader aware of the type material we have more generally suppressed in the interest of readability and clarity in the present work —Ed.]*

So who cares? When the frieze of draconic rulers and gory sacrificial stories is finally sorted out, the Lost Greek Apostles, the Later-day Saints Ephen and Em, along with Trixi, will survive.

A dozen greased and bechrisomed and charismatic Sons were probably born and anointed on earth in the same decade on the cusp of the Aquarian-Piscean Ages, but we monotheistic bionuclear sages think of only Our One. He was—they were—possibly but one of many phenomena of that other ancient New Age, as are the events

*here now in our own New Era. And the same sequence of happenings
probably occurred elsewhere on other continents dozens of times those
eons ago, and since, and perhaps do now as well.*

*There are surely acres of asteroid craters, star-master traces and
raster-race celestial cart aces, especially here in the immense but long-
so-parochial Rainbow Subkonfedo of Suda Kornukopio, where the
lore of heroic caretaker He-role/She-lore grew so rich and rapture-
wrapped and the spiritual ore bore was so untapped even before those
intense interstitial Interspell Years. There was no pretense, no sense-
of-history here, and no one paid heed to much that was happening
among the old self-righteous kooks and their floods of genetic foolery
and bloody psychic cuckoldry.*

*Remember how Louie Meershelrook flew to California at the
behest of that Jesus-guy bum who stopped by to pee in 1930-something?*

And as Science starts over now, reverently, the reconciliation
of evidential discrepancies can really be left behind or set aside,
for the glimpse of multiple anthropocentric truths is worth the
effort to stretch our minds to trace and embrace a newly etched
Sketch of It All. *¡Dios!?*

I suggest it is the circumstance of time and place and not
the fickle flickerings of the trite primetime limelight that are
important. Perhaps if the strange goings on in 1920s Heventon
and in California too had but been heeded, the rest of the world
might have been a century ahead, and not become so dreadfully
needy and out of sync on that temporal brink and fork awhile
back.

But I am only the two-fisted West-Wind-smitten advocate
and *ad hoc* witness to what I have written about, and I can tell
only my own story, enriched by my lucky contact and pact with
plucky Sarah, who played out that so laureate a role and bowled
us over with such an ornately whole and packed creative but
cracked urn or crock....

And I recognize that, as chronicler—perhaps as chronic
quackery herald and snake oil tonic extoller — I become part of
the imperiled fetish promo that meshed with that mighty Hug

Slut, Time (in the traditional sense), and started to take up the pliant lag and slacken the plague during these several generations.

And then of course finally it really did *jump ahead* just as it had a generation or more before for those few in the Ford Trimotor *Rubicon* while we re-amassed forces, reassessed the players, and gave a go at it, bringing in at last some new fun casts and acts for Another Run For It, fitting in more funky characters, rewriting in rap the ripped and cryptic layers of script and bringing it all up-to-slippery-date, until the final thrust when the unjust Old Era and its feral forces started to combust—the final last descent at the end of a long trend—but still too long before that glorious lusty morning when the New Era was finally victoriously born and the combined manifestations of various seers made their booming contribution and zoomed on methodically to the Upper Room.

Chapter 24

Good and Evil

3D implies hidden surfaces, that is, "une part maudite"
(Bataille), the devil's part, which will always be unknown.
There is never light without shadows, nor life without death,
as in the Baroque world.
—Philippe Codognet (*Artificial Nature and Natural Artifice*,
Université de Paris 6)

The question of Good and Evil,
positive and negative,
animal and vegetive
plus and minus
would-and-should
(these misunderstood primeval dichotomies)
occupied me for a period when,
just before my early 50s,
my weird revered and bearded
wraith appeared, and
I found my (eighth?) "New Faith"
after my second
(or third, upon my word!),
spiritual *re*birth.
Oh, yes, I reappeared!
And what I learned in that clichéd rehashing

was—that "everything will be all right"
as long as we grow
and don't fight the flow
and know that, *as above, below;*
—that if we strive
to love even the worst,
and try to thrive;
—that isotropic and isotopically esoteric
vertices, tenons and mortises
of scoped hopes that scoop and loop
through hoops of strife
in benevolent verses and rhymes
are positive; and
—that we live in a
(mostly) benevolent universe,
where in any case,
the xenon-trace vortices
and age-old canon treatises
of positive forces
are more prevalent than the negative
malevolent curses,
at least at this worst rebel level
of the Universe
where we wait in that holy copse
before the festive and fictive
portico fresco,
the helix pro-hole
whop-chopper porthole
to the span-end rhythm of time.
This was hard to swallow
after the old Mushroom Era clouded over,
but we wallowed and then waddled mellow out
of the fallow marsh at the end.
And this was coupled
with the serenely untroubled

double doctrine that
although much is concealed
more will be revealed.

matrices (2-dimensional objects)
        and
                vectors (1-dimensional objects)
——Codognet (*Artificial Nature and Natural Artifice*, Université de Paris 6)

The attempt of our logical, unseasoned
literal reasoning thought proceedings
to artfully shape out
that part of "reality"
our pretentious senses tell us about
into an undivided vision
of the whole creation fission equation
seems to me as awkward as
stalking and wrangling a standard
old wire coat hanger
(that balky daily triangular failure,
with its dexter or sinister spiral and hook)
and trying to redesign it and bend it
into a fine sphere or ball,
to embrace It All,
like a trace of some graceful cosmic fractal lace;
and shear or spear,
ensnare and ensphere
a certain space in a Dali duality.
Indeed, though we might think we see
the full and total modality
in a perfect sphere of reality,
we can never grasp all of the ball.
And the few points at which the
bent iron wire may essentially be tangential
to the imagined sphere-interface whole

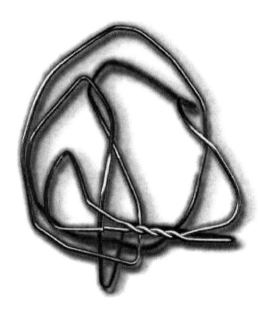

may well be part of what we so tirelessly pursue;
but most of the interlaced ferrous filament
will find only a ruefully partial and officious "truth,"
an orificial and artificial if aura-faced element,
and cannot touch, much less embrace,
that imagined perfect fundament place
that lies as it does out there in open space.
We try to define and fit reality in with this,
but we interweave only severe and rough
wiry angles and ugly curves that
won't ever reveal the real surface
and, no matter how we seek to wind and twist
and refine the wire crook, we'll never align our mind
with the goal we're aspiring to find or
bind the whole morphed gyre onto any "Sapphire Orb."
But the debased and defaced coat hanger

may still retrace and encase some trait of reality
as though it were a hollow, transparent spiritual
commonality,
and let us "see through" it and give us some vague notion
of what lies at several sparkling points
on the far hidden side of the sphere-in-motion.
But take heart!
That easy-squeeze golden figure of a
hooked and dangling hanger triangle
is, alas, the graceless face
of our tragic baseless logic,
as we travel through the mangled synapses;
grasping for "thesis + antithesis = synthesis,"
a remarkable human ability
that yields only hopeless abstract frozen stability.
And it is here someplace that the Qabbala fits in,
based on dangling entangled triangles, and more,
displaced, interlinked and overlapped
like a closet of tangled colorful hangers.
We can, of course,
deny the Evil Force and Jive
in the microcosmic phantasma
of our own tragicomic lives,
(and what else is there?)
if we "do the math,"
suppress the wrath,
Take The Right Path,
and know that when
Things Don't Go Our Way
and flow towards the goals
we've conspired to reach,
or follow our prior misguiding desires,
and we've strayed from Our String,
our spinal Swing and spiral Spring,
it was not Things

that were All Wrong all along,
I say.
We have a remarkable capacity and tenacity
and the divine audacity
to shun the bad and mad,
moon the fun son, the mad lad and the sad dad,
change direction, inflection and genuflection
and Find The Way: The Connection.
But the problem I had
with Evil, and "bad" people,
was that at least on the secular
side of the fence,
in a worldly and earthly sense
I doubted that it worked out
that for *everyone* there was no devil,
nor that we need not arm against harm.
Hence the notion of
—What, forgot?... Hot plot here!—
Two Worlds:
with one an overlay on the other,
the Negative "wrong" a weaker one,
while the double-strong
Positive rises, superimposed,
exposed and towering,
over the cowering loser.
So two good pluses and one bad minus
still maintain the valence and the balance,
And it is hard to explain in my own brash
scheme how all the mocking cosmic
and comically ironic cycles come to mesh,
and how lost long spells
sat trashed in the black back Gaps, before
that interstitial Interspell gash brought a
sonic bind and agile warp of fragile time
into that kind of Global Thorp;

when a tectonic ionic overlap
of two pixelated harmonics measures:
canted the fault and tilted the slant.
But does it matter?
Heavens, 11 dimensions?
7-come-11, or
13-spring demo-dementia guitar
roll-o'-the-dice?
Whither, 30-string Zither thing?
24/7 swings! Twang!
The ashen crash of time?

My life has, then, come full-circle, as I say. I complete the good things I dreamt of in childhood, often not, alas, until the third or fourth wild listing turn of that spiral cosmogonal gyre and twisting blast in my badly scattered gray matter, however clever I am.

Like my grandfather George Ludwig whose flesh I fill out and whose dreams I will still try to fulfill, till the end, I am a Piscean; though, like him, I cannot swim, and I have always been fascinated by air. I long wanted to fly.

With but little oil, and still no good substitute, the highways and railways and the commercial air travel situation fast became unraveled well before the end of the Old Era, and due to The Wars, natural disasters and ghastly anti-terrorism measures and pressures (more than the terrorism itself), the so-long-feared vast overcrowding of the now-always-cloudy skies did not come about.

So I gave in to my burning, got an age dispensation and learned to fly. For I knew that I would be in Nova Washingtono a lot during The Interspell, and I yearned to risk it all,

finally roar and soar over the great plains and drained lakes,

explore the slaked river deltas and more salutary tributary systems,

the drilled foothills and filled-in rills
of the ancient Appalachians,
the marred and scarred crags of the Rockies,
that ever-present Giant Lake Erie Rubber Tire,
the main chains of Ohio moraines and the grounds and
bewildering ghosts of Mound Builders,
bison, and toothèd beasts....
Serpent Mound. The Blue Hole.
All those old things Professor Whipple taught.
The Green Line.

Where was George Ludwig
between his death and my transfiguration,
on which cybernetic High Heister-Star;
what word the clue to his thunder,
what sound his light,
elixir his flesh,
and when, indeed, did he
—that male sphinx onyx shrub of the
burning umbilico-sphincter—
squeeze out the firey rood flare,
o Pensator?

[Pensator: D's secret *Auracrucian* name, received at his ordination. —Ed.]

Chapter 25

The World, etc.

Yes, again, finally, on those last strange, lonely
afternoon walks into the evening,
in barren, battened down
and flattened out Manhattan fields,
now the New Mews-Manhattan Emerald compound,
finally shielded from the fear
that had flooded and drowned
the battered shores
towards Staten those bloody years,
and from the slowly encroaching waters,
behind the dikes
under the straying rays of
bright failing yellow light,
against early bice-blue-and-gray sky,
as we'd enter the now-blighted site,
Sarah would take me and C
on the caballo-trolley
gaily galloping over
to that tilted North,
and as usual she'd pump us
to agree when she'd say of her magnetic compass
"It still works,"
as the needle ceased briefly to spin 'round,

but my hearing was bad
and this time I thought she had finally said
"It's still worse."
In any case,
Magnetic North had been displaced
and thenceforth ill-definedly misaligned,
and this had strange and bizarre
anomalous results.
For instance, the sparse few
of those farcical new
gasless adult autocarts
that still ran and might enter
the sector toward the Mews center
would be trapped, sapped,
enwrapped, and entwined
in a sort of vortex,
in the grasp of a fine-grid
magnetic maelstrom.
The New Mews-Manhattan Emerald city
was part of Sarah's ambitious scheme
to solve the world's problems
of mob slums, slob dumps
and dying sod clumps,
and dare to herald, yet another
fantastic but imperiled new world,
in a way evocative and reminiscent
of that idealist White City and Ferris Wheel
there at the 1890s Chicago World's Fair
and even more that provocative New York shrine
to science back in '39,
the Trylon, Perisphere and Helicline.
      And her dream to find some
real but Superhuman Ethereal Beam,
perhaps spawned by an Earthly MasCon,
[mas-con: a massive concentration of high-density material beneath the surface

of the moon or the earth —Ed.]
    became an eventual
    pseudoscientific theme
    of those Supreme North Astral dudes,
    and eventually the oh-so-spiritual
    Dixie Trixi Mascot Team,
    throes and bumps, mud and floods and all.
    Everything in this prized manmade
    Mews-Manhattan Emerald arcade
    had been miniaturized and downsized
    by the mad sub-stratum alliance
    of atom data and frantic genetic science
    first envisioned and then shrewdly and sagely abandoned
    those long ages before at the old Heventon MEWS.
    And alas, through the despised gene-agent
    recombinant developments that beckoned
    in the later pre-Interspell Years,
    the elite human hunks were also shrunken,
    in a kind of cloning or dwarf morphing stunt.
    It wasn't all as complicated and calculated as it may sound,
    but this was indeed Sarah's preposterous idea
    to eradicate hunger, and it was all predicated
    on the notion—as one might have guessed—that,
    as she said, "Little people ingest less."
    Fortunately, it all hardly matters now.
    That Sarah Siegfried Spiderman, all the while keeping her
true master designs and plans to herself, could have wreaked
the destruction (she called it recycling) of such a massive area in
Manhattan—not rivaled even by that vast and cruel earlier nine-
one-one fast-fuel dual shaft-reduction disaster in twenty-aught-
one—is evidence enough of her stunning power, and testimony
and tribute to her all-devouring cunning.
    What Sarah had not anticipated, of course, as she had not
heeded advice about some of the problems, even before the dikes
were built, was the dissipating effect that the Mas-Con magnetic

sphincter field she created there in the granite surrounding the Emerald Mews grounds would have on that veering and frenetic genetic engineering carried out at the project, and the resultant pathetically mutated Mews Estate Children,

because the moody soon-to-be overwhelmed
broods of a new crew there in the Mews realm,
born prematurely but precocious and near physical maturity,
were far from agile and indeed quite fragile,
misunderstood and vulnerable to
macing, chase and physical attack
by the larger and ruder bum-charger
slumhood base of the Old Race.
Also, of course, in the cloning zones in far dens
of the Mews Gardens, new germs
had grown to term,
sadly, radically changed,
just as predicted but gladly abandoned
long before at the old Heventon MEWS,

and the large dust particulates that plagued the Mews Gardens seem to have been charged in such a way that they remained suspended, ascending and descending and swirling about in unsteady aborted circular eddies of sorts.

Eventually, the milder, short, riled up and beguiled miniclones or childpeople had to be evacuated from ground level and kept in some of the once grand but now disheveled and glum highrises that remained in the area, barely inside the kinky new Manhattan magnetic sphincter ring.

Yes, after the Mews Emerald Gardens grew stranger
and the dangers were assessed
the miniclones were led like sheep
to the higher old Chrysler spire
and the newly gilded former Pan Am Building
(which still had a gyroport of sorts)—
in anticipation of the completion of more
of the new medically hermetic

bacillus-proof garden homes and villas
that would mirror those old London "mews."
From time to time a few of the trusted ones
were allowed to climb down to the much-feared
and purportedly "cleared"
(but still not dust-free) garden area
for an ardent *feria,* but then they'd nonetheless
turn up with distressing hysteria and
sometimes-fatal new sneeze diseases,
wheezes and other rosy petri-tripe
rip-snorter respiratory disorders;
and even minor abrasions
would be followed by large-scale invasions
of those robust pollen particles, dust particulates, and so on.
Fortunately the Mews Children were sterile and
would die out at an early age.
But it was the battle Sarah had to wage
against ageless insects that raged
in the garden park that finally
took all her energy, sparked
the decline and marked the near total fall
of her personal, physical
and financial recourses and reinforcements,
which is to say they led to serial material losses
and nearly exhausted
her international industrial resources
except for those she had invested
in the New West.

The shattered miniature world of the New Mews-Manhattan
Emerald Gardens was originally conceived to survive without
oil, raw materials
and crude energy,
but the concerns about burning fuel
that so pervaded technology

into the extended end-fade
of the Old Era
was no longer a portending problem,
or was, at least, dwarfed and warped,
moored and wharfed
by that other deep-fissure issue
that may never be dealt with:
the creation of all the new
thought-to-be-wonderful
but defective chemicals that had
such devastating, unsuspected,
unexpected, early-undetected
and unabatable,
rotten and unchecked
karate pop-chop effects
and rife and unforgiving
whopping bopper whacks
on life proper
in this overpacked old terrestrial tract
on which we have but a bivouac hold.
Here in a troubled
divine-slice of our
once blissful roll-of-the-dice paradise,
the songs Chiron taught us
are mired
in the sounds of the Siren's
Viral Call to our environs that is
vectoring and hectoring us in the direction
of a Second Reckoning
of the spectral and funereal,
now double-pierced periphery
of our thinning earth bubble cloister,
in general.
   Reports of bizarre events there in the isolated Mews, though
frequent, were so obscured in the news of general wars, the heat,

flooding, chaos and bleeding violence and change of the day, that they were totally ignored. Thus, little attention was drawn by evidence of mutated, albeit thus-far benign sports, friendly scutated and fatted rats—or *ratonoy [large rats —Ed.]*—decadent, lewd, careworn, sodden, hound-like and downtrodden, which, rattled by their ordeals in the highrise towers, toddled and waddled around up and down the scary back stairs.

Word came also of tiny feline beasts called *katiloy* that were survivors of a Mongolian Ice Age, discovered live in China after that third epidemic just before The Interspell. But as the jaded public began to focus on the pseudoscience and spiritual guidance of Dixie Trixi and the changing sociopolitical climate, little attention was paid to these diminutive cats, which were viewed as testy pests mostly because they were so small, evasive and pervasive that they often went unnoticed when they escaped through a breach in the Mews and took over other locales.

And now as well, foundling fauns and mini-hippogriffs frolicked among piny peonies in the tiny "horticourts" of the Mews Emerald Villas.

But all this began to pale before the unsought and unfought Insect Onslaught, as I said.

In any case, the New Mews-Manhattan Project would be totally abandoned and closed in The Interspell, bringing with it the decline and near abandonment of Manhattan, as well as what was called the Great Tramontane Dispersement, the second massive move to The West, but that is another story.

And the now-flooded Healing Camps at Forts Picket, Lickett and Dix, near Deep Pit, New Jersey were replaced by some remote Kern County hot springs in Centrala Kornukopio, where uraniaum was found in the steamy spring vapors and even in the air, to be absorbed through the skin or even breathed in.

On the positive side, the fossil fuel paradigm was about to meet its inevitable fate, with technology long suppressed by the embroiled oil royals, the voter-promoted motorcar makers and the late once-petroleum-funded Presidential Dynasties—the imminent harnessing of gravity forces, etc. (How easily it slides off the tongue!)

And by the time the unfinished Mews closed down,
the dikes had been breached
and old Manhattan had declined and fallen,
the problem of energy and the reliance
on fossil fuel had diminished.

Although Sarah once viewed most of what she had until then achieved in her life as merely the groundwork for the New Mews-Manhattan Emerald Gardens, her isolated pilot island model for the New Era, she actually accepted its failure stoically enough.

Curiously, even Sarah came to see, as it is so often in life for us all, that doing the redeeming footwork we believe necessary for the ends that seem desirable
   may seem
   a two-forked trot
   to an uncorked
   cock-shot snort of
   quark vacuums and torques,
   but this does lead towards growth and change,
   the most important part.

Ah, how we rarely succeed in our purportedly holy and extolled but greedy old goals. No, it is best that we cede the way, leave the final end unachieved and accept what we get, I believe, and
   let what's undone be later seed, to breed greater good deeds.

In Sarah's case, the goal, the Emerald Gardens, failed, but that debacle entailed also New York City itself, and this would let Angelus Eden prevail in the West, as she built other isles in Suda and Centrala Kornukopio, in the salty Slanto Sea and Nomo Lake.

...but I get ahead of myself. Again.

It has also turned out, of course, that the magnetic force field Sarah had imperfectly tampered with had other even more complex effects worldwide, and beyond, and the earth's whole Mas-Con field was actually itself vexingly adrift and shifting and needed to be revamped and things "set aright," as Sarah said, for the Mews-Manhattan encampment evidently had assumed a new role somewhat analogous to a skewed North Pole.

And, what's worse, it appeared also that there was already an at-first-barely-perceivable, perhaps resultant, said some beleaguered consultants, unfavorable excessive precessive wavering beyond expectations from Earth's uncertain 23-plus-degree inclination that might actually tip or dip the globe even more without warning, just enough aberration for acceleration of a perceivable further climate change. A few dared vainly hope that this would counteract the persistent warming.

So, as earlier scientists had correctly predicted, the earth orbit also became more unstable, and the magnetic rift and "gravity lift" somehow swiftly shifted the distance between Earth and her superb Luna. This was all coupled, of course, with a slowing of the earth's rotation, making clocks at best less than precise and standardized time a matter of confusion and dispute. Not to mention the unceasing increased tidal motion and encroachment of approaching oceans, the mud and the flooding.

A remaining straggle of scientists reasoned that seasons would change even more violently than they already had and range wildly, tides would rise and fall as never before, and the forces of nature would be charged to produce and embrace a biological revolution, the evolution needed to cope with the new conditions, and so on.

Ultimately it took a score of renowned minds, perhaps the Hand of a Bountiful God, and a great deal else, it appeared, to conceive a plan—still to be fully achieved—to steer and veer the magnetic Pole around.

Among those summoned to the *Dua [Second –Ed.] Supera Konfabo,* called at the last minute by Hakem von Funk, there again in Venice, where the Retrococo Foundation had become Postcyberpunka Fondo, to lead the way and deal with the somber and macabre geophysical problems Sarah had created, were a number of us *[nota bene –Ed.]* who also resolved to guide Sarah, at last, onto some spiritual level of acceptance, for she had finally had some kind of Revelation through all this mess, it seemed, and become willing to abandon Mews-Manhattan and all that might entail.

So, led by Dixie Trixi and his expanded Decemviri, including Hakem, Eb, Trixi, and Saints Em and Ephen, W.K. Morosi out of Synesthetica, the Buell Bantu Group, James Krusoe of The Bath Foundation and a host of others, plans were approved to assist that at-last-uncertain Sarah in readjusting the old "North Pole" mas-con and move her steadily ahead toward the New Era she had begun to dread because she was no longer quite sure where she herself was headed. She at last accepted help and embraced the shattering beginnings and spinning underlacings of an auto-pop-up Utopia, along with those patterns, schisms and cataclysms embodied in the iota-bop Dixie Trixi Emanations chatter.

And incidentally, the disorganized but sometimes effectively destructive Jesterson Trio had assisted in further sabotaging communications that had long before started to fail.

Problems had first been generated
by the interaction and confluence
of many different factors, including the crash
of lofty, poorly initiated and unchristened computer
software systems.
Those early-21st-century greedy and dishonest deceptions,
along with the enormous costs of military debacles that
together toppled the wobbly gargantuan financial blocks
and targeted the global markets,
were the first glaring glints and hints
that perduring crisis was taking root underfoot.
And an abundance of
custom number-cruncher computers

at major investing houses had repeatedly blundered
and spread the lousy germ,
causing chaos in the far-out securities mart,
selling blocks and bundles
of the same stocks of worthless stuff,
doublecrossing even the rough-and-tough,
and precipitating heavy losses
in the enlarged margin markets.
Not surprisingly, the reaction to this
was out of all proportion
to what the distortions of facts
should have demanded
and led to the calamitous
and disastrous racket pacts
and criminal acts
of those fearful "Black Octobers"
well before the Year Alpha,
and successive maelstroms of failures
far exceeding the rumbles that began as far back as late 2008,
along with the rupture, fracture, crack
and substantial screwing
and skewing of the whole trapped
capitalist financial structure.

Natural Forces, Too

It is perhaps unfair to blame everything that happened on
Sarah, nor to credit her with it all either, for the increasingly
frequent appearance of garbled gibberish on her new Vidi-World
Web can be partly blamed on
a sort of blighted stream
of bright and hot Sun-spit beams,
the famed solar-spout
blot-out flames that
came to befall us again and again

well into The Interspell.
And it is true that those damned spots
were out-and-out
the most severe,
mean and clean
shots since the last post-Pleistocene
green warming bash.
Fortunately, although these were frightfully chaotic,
they also proved to be periodic
and the erratic interludes
eventually diminished in amplitude.
But in the meantime all old and newer "nets"
flashed and almost fell and crashed,
like a toe-jammed Trojan Hearse,
and then as well
—fire, flail, fearful bane and wail!
bubble, bauble, toil and wobble—
communications and
information-storage
facilities and utilities
were randomly foraged,
turned to mush and porridge,
blurred and interfered with
by rolling deterrent multipolar
magnetic turbulence
and, again, those intermittent
solar disturbances.
And it seems not an unlikely supposition
that the bulk of the effects of the wild
skulking and finally hulking disruption of the whole
fret of electro-communications, multiple "nets"
and satellite webs that came so quickly
and crassly to become unstable and nearly disabled,
were also compounded by Sarah's data corruption programs.
For she was able to "core-correct" (her verb)—actually

"corrupt"—information stored in trillions of sources with a single hyperkey stroke in those vast interconnected and intermingled information webs and "nets" of the artful rat-maze trick-mix matrix she had concocted and stitched together starting subtly long, long before the last-ditch Internet pitched, retched and twitched in a final unassisted twist; not to mention its and her roles in the undeterred stir and unfolding blur, the bending, trashing and rending to ashes of the old Goofel and her new Floogle data base caches, changing sums and multiplicands; introducing meaningless real numbers where integers had been inferred or predicted.

One game Sarah played with delicious relish and hellish and splendid abandon, before what she described as the "failure and fall" of the inflamed Internet, was what she called random "jamming" of archives, the blind, mindless and perduring embellishment and introduction of pure fiction and significant and plethoric scientific contradiction, forced and channeled into specific annals of historical source materials, technical journals, and virtually all the electronic media on that old World Wide Web, so reliance on the speedy retrieval of accurate data was met with shattering disaster.

In the face of all this, Sarah found it easy to fleece the gullible and take over the old World Wide Web and Internet and rename it all Magi-Net and Vidi-World Web, and she falsely claimed to have cleaned it up and tamed the destruction of what she naively called "World Knowledge."

Moreover, what was called at the moment the Silicium Chip Disaster was certainly of Sarah's doing. The Jesterson team had infiltrated that major outdated and overweight computer chip developer and created a super-fast component blaster, which, it was realized all too late, was randomly inaccurate in some of its more complex calculations—just those irksome harrier-stratum areas and Zapapedia data chasms where rarer errors were hardest to detect and eject but which had far-reaching effects and slow domino-doomed snow-moon mood-balling and -altering consequences in the fractal world of dreg-and-dross ring-toss chaos and pathos—coupled with the so-called scabrous "Iris Bouquet" of computer viruses.

Through her own new Floogle "master access" to the morass of all the major knowledge treasures, using what she called the "defect averaging effect," she could revise, refract, contort, and distort even the most trivial fact or blast unmeasured vast amounts of valid data and render them errata, often interjecting imperfect anagram jumbles and assonance messes and incorrigibly forcing bad rhymes.

Of course the unwary who questioned the factual accuracy and sprawling faulty foolery of the various sprawling "nets" (who can keep track of them?) or even suggested that the baited knowledge tools in the Netbank Fret, Floogle and Vidi-World pools broke all the rules, were made to seem airy and drooling stoolies—even though they might have once done actual contrary research themselves—because the distorted "facts" were reported everywhere the same.

Sarah had taken great pains sometime before The Interspell to copy as much of what remained of the old already corrupt data onto her limited-access Vortexanet and even her superprivate Alteranet which used the old Teranet earth-girdle grid technology, thus preserving, she thought, a separate "copy" of all of what she called the "World College of Knowledge" at a particular moment, which she proposed to make available to only a select few of us, but then this apparently became corrupted as well, for, one day she went to that private net, and was met by this obscene message she later termed a TouretteNet Invasion:

Clock-tick and tom-cock dick ruse: come cruise and spurt comet r-ectum sop, spur the mute corpse mate copter corpses and copses into the poseur costume superstomp metro cusp cure for the muted museum corps: hoc est corpus meum.

Pocus cute, poke-pick pock-us romps, smut rip scrotum core and rust wreck-'em sputum symptom septum rectum spectrum, sperm spore erupt, stamp the scout romp muppiecorset and sport and pour the durn "Stirm and Dronk" tome to me. ¡Tome, hombre!

Fortunately, Sarah Spiderman had early-on viewed the World as Chaos, and she, long before others, voiced her notions that *really* nothing was any more predictable than the capricious weather and that even the most vicious climate could be affected by the tiniest fiddlings and meddlings in unrelated affairs—and here she found solace and hope to cope with The Warming, etc.

On my personal level, in sum, I find it is no longer possible to determine when anyone was born, for any dates that might still be found are bound to be suspect, and there is a particular dearth of data on births, much less deaths. Thus, many of our own players in this tribal tale are delphically described even elsewhere "in the literature" as being precocious or elfin, with the "manchild" handle and concept surfacing more than once; and some are credited with having sleuthed out and found some sort of Truth or a Fountain of Youth, a fleeting, provisional or at best transitional condition only delaying the end decay. Like Ideth and Sarah herself, others had multiple "Transitions," shrouded and abounding in and clouded by a chain of mysterious happenings accompanied by a range of strange trappings, with no physical remains, trace or stain ever found, perhaps flipped or slipped into one of the Gaps; only to then perhaps one day rip back and reappear in some later year.

The pleasures Sarah once found in clowning around in Mews-Manhattan town and garden had long since turned into burdensome, lamentable physical torments and her already long-blighted sight had finally failed terribly.

She had been fitted long before with one of the more successful ScanNerds for reading, but she did nothing but complain and had weirdly vulgar epithets for the contraption. She eventually spent 170 million *konfeday dolaroy* on research for "artificial vision" (which she somewhat unfortunately dubbed "Artifision") and other billions on efforts to compress and expand time.

Although Sarah was still not in the least released from her earthly caper or anything like deceased, by the time she moved to Burndale to work in her Scientific Institute for the Study of Time (SIFTSOFT), she may well have planned, in a grand last stand, to disappear, or perhaps totally "escape" this dimension.

I have thought that Sarah's final "disappearance," or "Transition," as we pretentious Auracrucians still call it, might well be a real slip into another slick slant o' time, but of course that is, I suppose, by some definitions, a kind of "Transition."

I see her there someplace reliving those amorous affaires of crusading Laddie Knights and Ladyes Faire—as the aging hairy red-headed kilt-clad Scot knight himself she wrote of in her novels Sir Hedon *and* Myrrh of Eden.

Sarah believed in time travel, and I can't prove that she didn't achieve it. The Institute for the Study of Time she set up to pursue this goal seemed to be near success, but of course it was destroyed in that Terrible Temblor, here in Suda Kornukopio. Some believe it was not just coincidence that the Institute was near the epicenter of that massive earthquake. I dare not speculate....

She was sure it was possible to track back and perhaps tack forward in time for at least short if abortive spells (a few days or minutes?) in the vortex shells and shields of the magnetic fields she created around New Mews-Manhattan and later in the mountains above Burndale; and although I believe she was a bit on the naive side in this matter, on the other hand, why not? And of course there were all those Gaps, perhaps localized, around New Blennerhassett and probably elsewhere as well.

"Time travel?" she once babbled. "The first step is to ravel the dates, 'Scrabble' the maps, then levitate."

Go figure.

It would be good to believe that clandestine genetic

experiments will not continue.

But the fact is that disregarded and all-but-discarded "Science," for all the tragic ecological and genetic terrestrial and pelagic disasters it has already wrought, has finally come to be seen as retarded and immoral Black Magick at this stage in our New Era, and opposed finally by the Global Quantization Council, which has already come to control, if not totally suppress, scientific research.

In fact, all the strobe-focal genetic probes,
cloning, coning and lobal gleaning, cleaning and reseeding
have led to a cunningly
conning naught of good, and indeed
to the creation of those fortunately sterile little miniature
beings; as well as the rise
of queasy and potentially destructive new species
in the cruel and dual domains of the
"aniplant" and "plantimal" kingdoms.
This has taught us, at last and
at least for the moment
("most of us," that is),
that we had, in
tampering with genes,
gotten to something
all-too-brazenly and -bracingly
basic, too fundamental to an anthropocentric universe,
to risk further tinkering with that old
"cosmic gear box," for, if the universe is in fact an anthropocentric one, and I am more and more sure that it is, as I've said, we had best not frantically tamper with the anthropogenetics.

Where is the truth (whose opposite is not an outright ruthless lie)?

Was it Gertie who started the *Dichter als Forscher* [*Poet as Scientist –Ed.*] notion, not the other way around? (A wolf-gang in Alice's closet?) [*Current references yield no evidence for a Goethe ["Gertie"?]*

*line containing, or work entitled, "Dichter als Forscher," nor is the phrase to be
found in the works of Gertrude Stein or Alice B. Toklas, but of course the source
materials are doubtless corrupted. —Ed.]*

Perhaps I am—these old bones are—
indeed the last of the clones
to come out of the old Heventon MEWS,
among those seeds in that pathetic
early go at genetics
long before the catastrophic revival
there in those last years
at Mews-Manhattan.

No, I can't get it out of my head, as I've said, how curious it
is that Grandfather George Ludwig and Bertha Zoetta, perhaps
fearing some unexpected outcome, should have left town for the
Wild West while I was in the womb!

Was I part of that outrageous page of MEWS history, the
"generation of '31," *[most sources place D's birth in 1927. —Ed.]*

born there in the old Work-Shop Cloning Compound,
precocious, complex,
pseudo-loquacious and slow to age?

I have wanted to check this out through a DNA analysis,
but must await the end of the strict moratorium and rationing
imposed by the Global Quantization Council on such
exploration, as well as the lifting of the apparent embargo on *any*
of my own further investigations.

But nonetheless, yes, Grandfather
lives in me, rather ensconced now,
right there where it counts,
truly undwindled as the undying dusky dew.

Chapter 26

The Trixi Revelations and Emanations

As the blurry, slurred blare and glare from the all-pervasive and invasive VisionSets became a more and more surreal stir, most of the now nearly deaf and stupefied pseudodyslexic masses were fitted with ear-implants or "EarLugs" to chatter with one another, near or far, or receive broadcast sound, and many also had small OculoPanners for both near and remote vision and what we used to call telecast reception. Some had advanced, enhanced and refined combined AudiOpticNodules implanted.

And they'd listen to or watch almost anything, so they were ready when those
"Trixi Revelations and Emanations"
that were thought so inspiring
came drumming,
humming and blasting
sometimes even through the plumbing
and wiring.
The masses got all spellbound and awed
by the new-found Dixie Trixi and his
pseudo-profound and seemingly exotic
hypnotic repetitions and admonitions
couched in flawed logic
and philosophical and scientific jargon,
that came through the ether with
probing spiritual phrasing, and in the bargain

actual practical suggestions as well as
discussions of profound questions that
trailed off into mindless blather,
reminiscent at times of those hallucinations
we (or at least I) experience when half awake
in the Theta Wave State.

And though there are among the remaining scientists and other professionals a covey of brazen disbelievers, the boundless and unfounded but amazing Revelations and Emanations of Dixie Trixi astonished and astounded a great number of naive and not-so-naive researchers, even some of the most astute achievers and truth-seekers.

I've compiled from various sources a sampling of "emanations" that have aired:

[Trixi speaks with a slight Southern drawl, all the while scrawling equations and diagrams on a sort of Illumaboard.]

That recent evidence of diverse life
not only on Mars
but elsewhere in the farther universe
must give you all pause, for it
caused an almost instant
re-evaluation of the stature and nature
of our now mature Man- and Wombkind and
the whole universe bowl and platter,
whatever!
We suffered, those old millennia through,
from perennial carnal guilt,
the instilled notion that we had sinned,
and we'd been chagrined, tilted and spun down
by those frilly and silly misguided
oracle pretenders and miracle benders
breakin' wind.
Awake and Hark, and Mark the Start!
Here's my spectacular probin' research concernin'

what I've called "the other Mo's"
—from the beginning and up to
the hand-me-down Moseses
and a few once-mob-mad mod Mohammads.
Yes, the twelve Secular Roses
and the Flight from the Pharaohs,
have given us new perspectives
on rising apotheosis theses, to wit:
Egyptian Rushes? Rustles in the Brush?
Mussels? Multiple Fissures and Multiplied Fishes!
Yes I've found a whole new force,
and I've been touched with a power that'll let them scholar fellers
out there make use of my soon-to-be-expected ability
to download and decode stuff into a kind of
neither digital nor decimal but fractal-hash analog matrix mode
that has brought New Meaning to Human Existence
and the extolled "Rule of the Holy Gruel" and our goals.
Am I not tight and right?
Reet! Join me, y'all,
gimme the hand,
follow my lead
in the Apollo Creed;
flee the stark hollow and the dark
mica-moat Fall and allow this
Call from The All, indeed an
A-Tomic Coma-Bleed Search
in the Atlas of Astral comma seeds
and factorial math-based,
cortical weed and comet artifacts,
to find the farcical mascara-staccato
smart-car Mars Cart <u>Mater Spark</u>

[He underlines the words on the Illumaboard.]

that mother-matter meter quark
as She mounts

to the aft Cosmic Fount
and Fraternal Altar of
Transplantimals and
Atomic Fractals.
Get it?

[Organ music swells fore.]

And to You Breeder Brethren,
and to even the sleaziest far-flung members of our species, in the
deepest, steepest and creepiest sick and poverty-stricken parts of
the once-wicked and -weakened world:
Greetings!
Congregate with St. Em and St. Ephen,
Kurt and Carson there in Dresden,
and the other holy brothers and sisters,
congregate and yes even conjugate in your local
meetin' and prayin' places
and hear the
True View, the
New Scriptures from the Other Spaces.
And you may want to buy and try my
"Rosy Teacup SoundBits"
that came to me from the Impeccable Mother Space,
to replace and throttle the mottled posies
and poetries of your hokey pocus sect,
pectoral-packed curate-eater poseurs.
Let them pun, make fun of and poke us,
hock us up with their hacked-up hocus,
but when all is said and done
we will overcome!

[He seems to lose his train of thought and mumbles:]

Yes, the brittle arse-bitten Holly-Goosed Father
is indeed tethered by a loose lint twine
in a Sen-Sen-filled bile-mousse tent,

while the long-hugged Son
is then aptly wafered-and-dunked,
crossed and wrongly lugged and hanged
in the old rugged acrostic juice.

[Now again in a loud voice:]

How 'bout it?
I say unto you,
The Music of the Spheres
is not all that far wrong a song,
for the gong-prone gang is
a strong and long-thonged ego prong
of It All,
an intense If-ication,
a "densifying pene-tration."
      And Expansion is the raving EMANATION-veneration
of hoppety-hip Zoroaster waves—
the last faster-and-faster blasting and
casting of the Soon-To-Be Past
into small image-rap casters among
ever vaster and unsurpassed
old preachers and pastors in the land of the Master Band.
But I rant?
And now it's time for y'all to chant:

uuuuòOOwn   uuuuòOOwn

uuuuòOOwn   uuuuòOOwn
etc..
So there I am,
take me or leave me:
a bad and sad rabid acrobat and actor?
your cardboard bastard
starboard ship bard
on this oratorical robot-shop
apostasy-rostrum trip

in a Palladium radiocast
that radiates Good N - E - W - S
to the four winds North, East, West, South,
drifting even to the Outer Other Ethers.
But the echo never totally disappears,
comin' back the long way 'round behind,
hyphen-siphoned and typhoon-churned
through an enlivened VisiFone wormhole,
a temporal spiral tempest turn that hugs back onto itself
through the endless-space
in the Sterno-lap of EternaPlace.

[He sings a verse from Glenn Miller's "Stairway to the Stars."]

The infinity of the Mighty
High-Knight Finite,
is right on!
So give me the high sign!
Hang 7, 24.
You better believe it!
You see, it's all so simple, predictable and Delphic:
what we have come upon is a cell flick,
a fleck of our own delicate selves
in the helical Ever-Connect
of our spheroid universe,
that shell of a relic donut void.

[He sings a verse from Doris Day's "Sailing Along Down Moonlight Bay."]

And without apology I dare proffer
that a datable creation seems more than likely,
though further back than 4-0-0-4 Before C.
And what of The Word? you may wonder.
Genesis innocence is not so absurd
in the Big Bang concept harangue,
and Pythagoras was mostly right

in reducing things to a numerical light.

And why do you so easily believe in The Tragic Disappearance and not The Magic Reappearance?

The whole resolution of the "death problem" has been acceptance of disappearance. If someone tells you his brother passed into Transition (as those heretical Auracrucians say) durin' the night, you will not question it; you fall into feigned or true empathy, sympathy or grief. "The Loss of It All," you say. But let someone tell you that his thought-dead brother appeared to him in the night, however, and you will greet him with inner disbelief, though you may politely cop out and opt not to show it. You can't go back in time, you think.

So much is so simple.

Take out pen and paper!

Write this down; it's almost all you need to know:

The word "GAN" —g-a-n—means any organized sphere of activity, a garden, a body, a world, a universe. The word "Eden"—e-d-e-n—means a time, a season, an age, an eternity, as well as beauty, pleasure, an ornament, an omen.

Yes, mark it well, those words Gan and Eden embrace and enlace It All — Time and Space.

Stick with me. Believe in my fitness to bear witness and you are saved with the final Word, the road to GAN-EDEN, the Clue to It All, what more do you need?

Oh, yes, and don't forget; write this down too:

"Gas means Empty Chaos!"

Now I'm gonna show you the Secret to It All, as that Stephen Hawking fella admitted and "spoke" so well back in 20-aught-four..

[Then he flashes on the Illumaboard, and we hear Stephen Hawkings' "voice" say:]

> **A black hole only appears to form but later opens up and releases information about what fell inside. So we can be sure of the past and predict the future.**

Those of us as old as I am found it hard to believe that the mobs and masses followed and swallowed all this, so I'm glad I'll finally go on into oblivion before such trivia take firmer hold.

But of course, there have been No More Wars, and things *are* looking up.

Chapter 27
Deep Stuff

So, now, because of the gyratory and hallucinatory conspiracy of my own at once both failing and revelatory memory, not to mention the dishevelment of my archives, and possibly several Time Gaps, I reiterate that we have to be satisfied with the slender little I have recalled and reconstructed of the illusory political intrigues, events and brawls that were to befall and even enthrall us and draw us all in, which led to the *Supera Ĉarto* and Trixi, and so much more. Once, again, this is the best I can do and it will have to suffice for the nonce in this agglutinative narrative.

I long believed that in politics, "Plus ça change, plus c'est la même chose" *[The more things change, the more they stay the same. —Ed.]*, and that Revolution serves only to punctuate and perpetuate the fluctuating Establishment. But...

What turns out to be more important and deplorable than the details of politics in this age entails rather the influence of the myriad electronic media sources and other more general physical forces, in confluence with the decline in the level of what was once thought of as liberal cultural education, and the rise of belief in the Trixi Emanations, accompanied by, to wit:

—the raising of the general "useless and extraneous-info quotient" of the individual because of the quantity and type of fake data taken in from the ocean of what is proliferated;

—the general decline in the ability and willingness of people to read, in particular during the last generations; as well as eventually

—the epic spread of DeciBox- and EarBlaster-induced deafness;

—the sounds that abound and surround us, and batter and shatter our hearing; and finally

—a sort of phototonus resulting from the waffling and throbbing light and pulsing glare of the reflective VisiGoggles and all-pervasive and repulsive KinetoShow IllumaPanels and ElectroScreens, leading to near blindness.

The major focal social changes I see are manifested in the division or twigging off of the human race into *Intelektuloy* and *Dronoy* *[Nova Esperanto: intellectuals and drones —Ed.]* that crested with widespread pseudodyslexia, that sort of inability to correctly connect consecutive bits of information, playing out as a saturated and concentrated attempt to absorb simultaneous bytes of extraneous data, the so-called "multitasking"—too much "input" all at once.

Then there's the not perhaps unrelated collapse of time. Everything occurs as a fuzzy subliminal streaming blur; there are no more "solids" and everything tends to nuzzle and blend and wedge in around the edges of the dreamy puzzle. Our perceptions are technologically induced; our "reality" is no longer tangible or "real" to us.

Not all that long ago we read by candlelight.

I posit, perhaps tactlessly, that these changes are more fundamental and of greater impact on our species than the genetic fiddling that has deliberately taken place, though I oppose that as well.

On the other hand, of course, some of all this brain change *may* be attributable to the direct effects of chemicals in our environment as well as "rays" from the Sun and Outer Space that rupture chromosome structure, but I think the ominous cerebral phenomena are more commonly just as much adaptive, selective evolution, which, reflecting the stacked impact it has already had now, will surely take its toll and play a later weighty role that will be hard to evade in future decades of the New Era, unless one ventures to suture the latent structural fissures within and without.

What seems to loom
changed and
rearranged
is the blooming
human spirit and
—I fear it—
the more mundane domain of
what remains of the
homo sapiens brain;
daily excited as it is far into the night
by that frighteningly bright light
that once seemed
—and was deemed to be—
so fine, benign, beneficial and esteemed; and
the hectic waves of electric rays
and emissions that radiate all over
and permeate the outer oval cover
of our own tightly woven gray matter.

And we must not overlook the polluted air we breathe, seething and imbued with both new and once totally taboo chemical brews;

and the ravages that reach us and leach us
through the ionospheric shield that so long
sealed and protected us, now infected,
and hopelessly broken and loaded
with carbon allotropes and a noxious oxygen.

Fortunately, there are now, finally, faint signs that the sleeping masses may awake from their stupor and evolve into some kind of *superay proletoy* [*sort of semi-professional proletariat classes —Ed.*], as all the cyberforces give way to what was once called "village" craft and nourishing culture.

Chapter 28

From D's 'Mémoires'

[Editor's note: In the manuscript I was given, this chapter was totally garbled and although I could have re-numbered the final chapters, ending with an untidy Chapter 29, I have instead included material from D's parallel unpublished 'Mémoires,' mentioned in my Introduction, that seems to fill the gap. Excisions (in the interest of propriety) are indicated, as usual, with ellipses [...xXx....]. We note that the style is much more reserved here in the 'Mémoires' than in D's other writing. It is an older, mellower D that we see here.]

There has been some difficulty getting to the manuscript these days for one reason or another. Sunday, for lack of sleep the night before; today, due to late rising. I do groan so, creak and doze off. I shall try again this evening, but fear that if I do succeed and work into the night, I'll only be unable to get with it again in the morning, or use that as an excuse.

Tomorrow is my birthday, and I'm not quite sure how old I am. The slippery decades are so unsure these days, and the way they've jumbled the alpha-omega designations in the interstitial Interspell have rendered it all the more confusing, not to mention the repeated renaming of the 13 months and the obliteration of all references to 21st century dates after around 2018, and of course the more recent changes in the length of days, years and moon phases, soon to be reflected in yet another new attempt at a 35-day-month system, they say. And how do I count the Gaps?

Holywood here in Angelus Eden is far from recovered

from the Terrible Temblor, the Great Burndale Quake and Fire that destroyed Sarah's Scientific Institute for the Study of Time (SIST or SIFTSOFT). And Sarah has not been heard from. Fortunately, though of great magnitude, the quake was apparently quite deep, and damage was not as widespread as had been feared from The Big One, if indeed that is what it was. Not unexpectedly, scientific appraisals have been hard to come by, especially since that world-famous earthquake study center at Kornuko-Tek Institute in Glendena, which had survived all the suppressive science cutbacks, was also destroyed. Fontanbloa Turo *[the old Fontainbleau Tower, the Holywood highrise where D had kept an apartment since the '80s —Ed.]* has survived fairly well, and the soot has been cleared. Fortunately some of the AutoGuyPods are still running and it is not too difficult to get around, but everything is still a mess.

In this erratic week I have not sat down at the Voxiwrite, where I still use an old keyboard I've salvaged, but I had hoped yesterday to reread or perhaps listen to the work I have now brought together in first draft, a scramble of words and ideas drawn, many of them, from scraps and notes, as well as some more disorganized file cards I scribbled the last time I had access to Sarah's archives, made available to me sporadically by her right-hand guy, Oscar.

Last night I was with Oscar, who had come in to Holywood from the Nomo Lake Complex. He is from the true Midwest—the former Kansas. He came to the then-Los Angeles when he was hardly 21, and I met him not long after, those generations ago.

[...xXx....]

[The relationship between Oscar and D was intense, but probably brief. D says elsewhere in the 'Mémoires' that he was influential in Oscar's becoming the chief aide to Sarah Spiderman Siegfried. —Ed.]

Oscar had fundamental skills in a lot of areas, and when it came to the basic planning of the Mews-Manhattan Emerald Gardens Project he quickly became expert in a dozen fields that had to do with the practical construction of the Project—and the dismantling and disposition of the buildings Sarah had been quietly acquiring, followed then eventually by his closing the whole thing down.

It was apparently his ongoing grief that brought Oscar to me in Holywood. He fears that Sarah might have perished, and his sorrow seems so deep and genuine that I would guess he is either in the dark about her death or disappearance or in on the facts but dramatically concealing them, even from me. In any case, despite the affection between us, which goes back these eons, he seems unwilling to give me access to her archives, now stored on that artificial Isle of St. Nola in the salty Slanto Sea out there beyond Hemet. Perhaps they did not survive, as I've heard the sea went dry during the earthquake.

His emotions are mixed, and he is clearly confused. He wishes so much that Sarah were "alive," but if it turns out that she has not "transitioned" but merely disappeared, of course that would mean that she has deceived him and used him. It has not occurred to him that she might indeed, in one of her SIFTSOFT experiments, have gone on through to...

"But it's all part of what she thinks of as her Great Purpose that she's gone; just wait, when we see her again she'll explain it all to us, and then you'll really understand why she had to do it this way," I say, trying to console him. His tears are on my shoulder.

[...xXx....]

Indeed, Oscar seems truly lost. He is now a handsome blond-gray-white-haired man. His sight has grown much worse than it was when I met him and they seem to be unable to fit him with implants, so he still wears the old-style heavy glasses, but he is most attractive in them.

I have tried one final time, this 25th day of Hallow of what they're calling Year N-7 of the New Era, to reach Sarah. I scan through, as they say, her A-code in the PowerSearch mode, available now only to some of us members of Alteranet, in the hope that a chink or cranny in her Netfaçade might open, but the result has come back with a variety of those archaic messages such as "wrong entry," "try again," "information not accessible," "protected entry, need key," "question out of order," and so on, as though it were some game.

In any case I arranged to meet Oscar again next week, in Heventon, to see if Sarah might possibly be holed up there, as there is nothing left of her compound in Burndale or even Glendena. And I want to try, once again, to get access to any of her papers from the early days that might still be there in Heventon.

Sometimes I privately wonder if the whole Mews-Manhattan Project was not just a jolly giant movie set Sarah had ordered constructed by Holywood technicians, thaumaturges and magicians, and whether the "Good N-E-W-S" contained in the Trixi Revelations and Emanations, et al., is not simply from some talented but perhaps deranged public relations team Sarah might have hired away from one of the major vid studios.

Though Heventon, home of the Wright Brothers, was long promoted as the air capital of the world, in memory of those inventers, it never became the hoped-for transportation hub, and today its air service is by somewhat indirect connections on infrequent or inconvenient random flights.

I no longer like flying, or travel of any kind, now that the *flapero [aircraft —Ed.]* terminals have become so dangerous, and the airfields so appalling. And the at-best-erratic service, with so little attention to schedules, is intolerable to me, even at my advanced age, when I am so patient. Not to mention the decrepit *flapero* and *pufero [another type of aircraft —Ed.]* equipment.

It turns out that C and E—C's new friend—both have to go to an African linguistics conference in Cincinato, some 80 kilometers south of Heventon, and we shall make a little holiday of the trip. (I'm so glad for the new Cincinato spelling... I could never get it right before.) Then we go on to what remains of the Esta Kosto *[East Coast –Ed.]* if we can get clearance, to visit old friends and make a last attempt to find Sarah if she is not in Heventon.

I really do want to visit Heventon, for it has been many years now, and I must satisfy myself as to whether Sarah might be there leisurely tending her rose garden, as it were, perhaps even in her sherry-cups, or at least sipping the "butter tea" she was so fond of, musing about the comedy she has written on the pages of human history.

E is gorgeous this afternoon and C coaches and coaxes, as we three *[...xXx....]* high up here in Fontainebloa Turo, with Folio bringing us juices afterwards. (Quartto has grown lazy; he deserves a rest anyway.)

The pace of my writing is picking up again, and concerns about the fate of Sarah are alleviated by this decision to flap *[fly –Ed.]* to Heventon. I am hoping that in a few weeks I can put an end to the final chapter of the story, or at least this first installment.

They've given me access again to some of the various "net" and Web sources, but any research these days has become so tedious, I wonder if it is worth it. All-Search and Floogle churn up such a muddle of related and unrelated stuff that they are almost worthless now, and the endless indexes are really useless messes.

Today, now, the "user" determines the information available by the form or substance of his queries, and thus creates his reality from what he is able to imagine to ask and the way he puts it, and then what he chooses to believe of the answer.

Chapter 29

The Trip to Heventon

Late Hallow, New Era Year N-7.

Neither C nor E had ever been to my birthplace, Heventon, Ohio, and E, though born in Europe, in effect had never been east of the Misisipio on this continent, or probably even the *Nevada Siero [Sierra Nevada —Ed.]*.

We decided to go there Thursday and spend the weekend exploring my old hangouts before I would go with the two in one of those *vertola flaperoj* to Cincinato Monday morning for their conference. I was presuming that if I didn't find Sarah, I could try to do a little paper research on Heventon history to fill in a last few gaps in this present narrative, and begin my next book. I am so weary of this one.

I heard there is still a "bookhive" there and even the remnants of an old "bukateko." I wanted to visit these as well as meet the new curator of the Merganser Foundation, reminisce and carouse about like the old ghost that I am in that city, all the while showing C and E the haunts of my earlier days, the secret halls and tunnels of the Heventon Art Institute, that bench, and more. But Sarah's Spirea Compound, like the Merganser estate, the MEWS and even the Merganser Foundation, have all disappeared.

It amazes me that I am still alive. Eb is now in the Fourth Age, and I've gone on, in one sense to the Seventh Circle. And where is B now? Briefly returned from "Transition" those ages ago, but then...

The words C and E and I spoke there in the cockpit as I piloted the old rental *flapero* back to Heventon mingle now with my own reveries. We were as one voice anyway, and we had said these same things to each other before, but never at this altitude and never on this "natural high," and never with such excitement and immediacy and ecstasy, conviction, finality and belief. I do not know who said what. Alas, truth be, I do not remember what was said. *[But this does not impede D from proceeding to tell us anyway. —Ed.]*

Ah, how the turn of the screw of time takes us not to our envisioned destination, which is a postulated Myth based on our limited imagination, resembling all-too-closely the present and the known. For the real destination is unknown and unpredictable and unknowable until we get there; and vastly different and better than anything we could have conceived or created.

> *Yet, we must postulate*
> *The End, the Goal,*
> *and move towards it with Purpose,*
> *knowing it is imperfect, elusive, and wonderful,*
> *not unlike the old gas storage tanks outside Lima, Ohio*
> *or near Seven Corners in frozen Minneapolis,*
> *—those ugly sights and foul stenches welcome landmarks,*
> *or benchmarks,*
> *life-marks on the Journey North,*
> *wherever it may lie—*
> *on to the Origins,*
> *towards the flat-lake bedlands*
> *tilled by immigrant ancestors, and Indians before them.*
> *Yes, an Outcome (!) vastly more desirable*
> *than anything we ourselves might conceive or direct,*
> *one that signals the end of a long, arduous journey.*
> *We knew that everything in this spiral continuum through*
> *space, time and the ineffable stuff of divine creation*

"comes full circle," as I have so long and often observed
in my seemingly-so-brief life. If we allow ourselves, we
can indeed really fulfill something like a childhood dream.
We can live out those Thomas Wolfe longings of youth
(the train North,
away from home, out of the pain?)
if we will let it all flow in the gods' way,
if we will be part of the
Kingdom and the Power
and the Glory for ever and ever.

Yes, It Was All True.
We Knew The Answer.
We knew it all had been worth it;
—that all our dreams had really been realized;
—that all our humble goals had finally been met, satisfied
and surpassed;
—that we were indeed some small part
of the Grand Plan;
—that we had played our bit roles; that we would never
be required to Go Home Again;
—that the moment we had arrived at was final and perfect
and penultimate and imperfect;
—that the pulse our hands shared on that old plane was
one, The One;
—that the force of our pressed thighs tight against one
another was God-given and mighty and the electricity that
arced our wrist-hairs divine;
—that we were all-powerful within the Sphere of our
Desirables, as we used to put it, and Powerless in the arena
of our Wants;
—that Fulfillment was upon us and that we had arrived;
—that we had in this moment Great All-knowledge—all
we needed—without the Nets, Knots, Frets and Naughts,
and that we would lose sight of it all another day;

—that it would not be Lost, and yet it would seem lost to us;
—that we would lose and pass and surpass,
live and survive,
last past the last passing,
give and receive,
succeed and fail,
be hot and cold,
have fear and faith,
learn and forget,
believe and doubt,
live and leave,
love,
and be loved,
know dark and light,
day and night,
strings and springs;
and then find again,
and believe that
One Act of Faith
annihilates Two of Doubt.
The old One-Two.
$3 + 3 + 3 + 0 = 10$

It was a wonderful flight we made in that rickety flapero, and
it reminded me of a trip I had once taken from New York to San
Francisco in the '50s aboard a DC-7 when the sky was clear and I
could see the earth from only three or so miles up, the whole way,
coast to coast. Every physical feature of our vast and still-then-a-bit-
untapped land spread out below, and now here again it was rolling
along under us, though from a different height, but "moving" just as
fast—or as slow.

This time I was not alone,
was never to be alone again,
whether C and E or no one or all the rest are with me,
and I was Going Home...

...Going Home: to all the past and all the future;
to a home I had never known,
a home where I had no family
and it was all family,
home to those who had inspired me,
and who had been
such Imperfect Instruments,
home to the hills and the rocks,
the moss and leaves of Fall,
and All the Rest.
And I had come to know
Spanish Moss... and Mistletoe;
and come home to
the Lilly of the Valley of My Youth,
planted in my mother's little garden,
her tears and finally my own, at last,
for her, Viola Lilly of the Valley;
found grief for a Pigmenio Barboa I never knew,
his pack hanging there from my barracks rafter,
Pig, bo, bar, men again;
felt the wonder and magnificence
of another's touch and power;
shared with M, W, B, Eb, Sarah, Oscar, C, E.,
seen my hopes realized,
understood that at my advanced age
I had contributed that little vital part,
and felt I was still to give something
in The Game of the Gods
in which I had been allowed to move a few markers,
where the Divine Cartoonists
had allowed me to do a few strips,
revealed The End to me,
and then told me to write the story any way I wanted,
that it would end the same anyway,
that it didn't matter now,

and that the End was not the Last Chapter.
I, Seth Pensator.

The lights were low in the *flapero* cockpit as I guided us through the night and eventually C and E and I fell silent and into a delicious breathing together and theta-state revelation, and total relaxation—I knew that our brain waves were as nearly in sync as they ever could be and what was in their mind and in mine, those inner and outer forces, was the same for the three of us, them, me, The Other or Us, and that it was a Holy Synthesis. Life was fulfilled. The Great Love Story, written over and over again; we were in the Land of Happy Dreams and would never have to leave it. We had always been there but did not know it.

At first, the Heventon Airport seems essentially unchanged since 1961, or '41 or for that matter '31, I suspect. *[Note change of tense. —Ed.]* It is still at Vandalia, north of the city, and one still has a view of a few ancient planes landing and taking off.

"Welcome to Heventon—the Home of Aviation." Also known at various times as The Gem City, and The Air City. I expected to see the phallic old windsocks that used to blow and shift atop the sheet-metal hangars at the airport of my youth, and indeed they still seem to be there.

We stay at the Biltmore Hotel, of the same vintage '20s Renaissance Revival style I remember, now painted a gaudy orange and pink, reconverted from public housing. There is a *Hamborguilo* where the Purple Cow Coffee Shop was generations ago. A lot of the rooms have been let out to indigent followers of Sandeep Ranjiit, who apparently now owns the hotel.

It is all quite hazy now, and I am having trouble remembering our nights there, the events of this wonderful weekend are so clouded in my memory.
What shrouds it?
What actually did happen?

The downtown section of Heventon is no longer clean and prim. The unisex bars tend to be north across the Great Miami River on Main Street, where there are still many remnants of the early 20th century. This area must be a double vortex, for it spills out powerful ultrazone synesthetic tones, the strongest *déjà-vu* laser cones.

The house we lived in on West Great Miami Boulevard is gone, and the area has a number of small liquor and drug stores, and several bath houses—one, so oft in my dreams, oddly enough now named The Blue Hole.

This section of the city north of the river has been called Old River Town, but the river is dry. Even in my days, one could nearly wade across it in arid Augusts, especially there by the YMCA, but it was deep enough much of the year to drown in. Now it has water in it only after the rare rain, despite the dam. The same is true of its tributaries, the Mad River and Wolf Creek, even the once-deep Stillwater. The city is honored with more bridges than it now deserves, or than it now needs, though the one depicted on the old school tablets *[see Chapter 0. —Ed.]* is gone.

The rumbling echo comes back of the swimming-pool in the Italian Renaissance YMCA, grotesquely repainted now Delft blue. It still hits the skyline with its smell of pool chlorine. And of course, still there on the opposite bank of the river in even more glory, is the Heventon Art Institute, with that marble bench, the young curator, where I, a soldier still... knees, or something. Oh, how I could never be *me* here! Again, the loss of it all!

Getting around has become almost impossible because of all the battered, useless old vehicles scattered about, inert. And the damp air this night and cold drizzle could turn to sleet or snow with a drop in temperature of a degree, even though this is unlikely in late Hallow. Or is it Hollymount already?

We have the luxury of a hydrogen-powered Walker Three-wheeler.

Oscar is nowhere to be found.

Chapter 30

The Negmatic Field

Memory. *Mémoire.*

So after a surreal three days tramping around Heventon, we head in the rented Walker Three for the Heventon airport at Vandalia. A late-Hallow ice storm has indeed brewed up, and we drive blindly, perhaps lost.

Driving that puffing three-wheeler across now icy roads and sleeted fields, we have gone astray, maybe circling the airport. There is that same haze I saw on the double-death pair of trips I made in the '60s when my mother and grandmother died, that winter. Where is that funeral home? I can't remember.

Where are we?

But then… there's the airport; it seems a shambles of what it was but three days before. The tarmac has been dug up, and the windcock [*sic –Ed.*] hangs tattered and limp.

No, we're not at Vandalia. Now it looks like the Old McCook Field. It's all a blur. McCook Field, dating from World War I, named after a Heventon hero, a dead aviator in a pale blue-gray flightsuit. The field had been on the northeast bank of the Great Miami River, near the now-desecrated old Downtown, but was too small for even the '30s early commercial aircraft and had been turned into a park and then after the Great Depression a giant slum housing project—now miraculously gone, and converted again to an airport. A new name. Proust-Bonplaisir

Memorial Field! Dead? New Heros, indeed!

Now I'm no longer at the wheel, and somehow the Walker Three has taken off, expanded, has three motors and we are above the airfield. I see now we are circling in on another small patch of land Just Across the River. It looks like the old MGM Studios in Culver City, before they were destroyed in that fire. There is a half-mile-long cyclorama backdrop—painted sky, and a variety of landscapes that blend into one another, from the Grand Canyon to Ohio hills; Dresden; the Chrysler Building, the Western Mesas, even the stratigraphic layers of the earth, and the Eiffel Tower. Is this that fantasy airport they never built on the *Île des Cygnes* in the Seine? Swans Way? Outfall. There's that Giant Rubber Tire At The Lake! And Pittsburgh!

I realize we've stopped in mid-air, perhaps to land again? Across the River? We hover. Nothing is moving around us, nothing is moving past, we are descending, again, or are we rising? Vertical movement in any case. There is a slight jolt, a vibration that goes through the craft.

C's cheek with its 18-hour softbeard, and E's bristles are against my face as we strain to look out into the morning.

Mists are rising from the river and the landing strip is short, is steaming. The Pilot says something that is not clear. *Magic Net?*

Up, up, up.

"We have now entered the Negmatic Field, we'll be home shortly," or something like that.

Ecstasy builds. Now we are among other passengers, and a whole crew is at the door to let us out.

Sarah is waiting; B, and all the rest.

End of the beginning.

Heventon!

- finis -

About George Drury Smith

George Drury Smith received his bachelor's degree cum laude (1953) from Marietta College (Ohio), with a major in French and Spanish and a minor in German. As an undergraduate he also studied in Europe for three years at universities in France, Spain and Germany.

In 1968 he started publishing the avant-garde literary magazine *beyond baroque*, and soon afterwards opened what is now known as Beyond Baroque Literary/Arts Center in Venice, California. This was incorporated as Beyond Baroque Foundation in 1972. He headed Beyond Baroque for more than ten years. It moved into the historic Old Venice City Hall in 1979, where it still thrives.

For more than three decades he worked as associate publisher for *The Argonaut*, a weekly newspaper serving Los Angeles suburban coastal areas.

He now divides his time between Hollywood, California and Amsterdam in the Netherlands, with a month in Paris every year. In addition to *The slant hug o' time*, he has begun writing what he calls his "memoires." He has also been working with Sophie Rachmuhl revising and editing a translation of her French doctoral dissertation on the Los Angeles poetry scene from 1950 to 1990, to be published by Otis College of Art and Design in 2013.

CPSIA information can be obtained at www.ICGtesting.com
Printed in the USA
LVOW120118190612

286665LV00005B/3/P